The Type-A Guide to Book Clubs

A Sunset Ridge Cozy Mystery, Volume 4

Elizabeth Spann Craig

Published by Elizabeth Spann Craig, 2025.

THE TYPE-A GUIDE TO BOOK CLUBS

First edition. December 2, 2025.

Copyright © 2025 Elizabeth Spann Craig.

ISBN: 978-1955395601

Written by Elizabeth Spann Craig.

Chapter One

S am Prescott had faced down a Category 4 hurricane, coordinated community food drives, and once spent an entire weekend creating a household management system that would make Marie Kondo weep for joy. Walking into a book club meeting with six strangers shouldn't feel this hard.

The problem was that walking into Twice-Told Tales and facing a room full of strangers felt harder than any of those things. Sam loved reading and loved the shop itself, owned by her friend Charlotte Webb (who had the best name for a bookstore owner in the history of bookstore owners). And Sam genuinely wanted to expand her social circle beyond her neighborhood and the agility training she did with her dog Arlo. Book club seemed perfect in theory.

In practice, she was the new person walking into an established group where everyone already knew each other.

Charlotte gave her an apologetic look from across the room where she was setting up the tea service. Sam smiled back with more confidence than she felt and clutched her copy of *The Memory Keeper* like a shield.

"Sam!" Olivia Stanton appeared at her elbow, and Sam nearly sagged with relief. "Sorry I'm late. I got talking at the food pantry. What did you think of the book?"

"It took me a few chapters to get into it, but after that, I loved it."

Olivia said in a low voice, "Good, because Margaret is going to say she hates it. Fair warning, she hates most of our picks. Don't take anything she says personally."

Before Sam could ask who Margaret was, Charlotte called the meeting to order. "Good evening, everyone! First, I want to welcome Sam Prescott, who's joining us for the first time."

Sam gave a quick wave. Everyone turned toward her with varying degrees of interest.

"Let's do quick introductions," Charlotte said. "Sam, I promise there won't be a pop quiz later. Olivia, you already know Sam, so no need for an intro there."

Sam pulled out her notebook, knowing she wouldn't be able to remember all the names without help. She'd catch the important details now and sort out the rest later.

"Taking notes?" Charlotte asked with a smile.

"I'm terrible with names," Sam explained.

"I think it's brilliant," Charlotte said warmly.

An older woman with steel-gray hair pulled into a severe bun spoke first. "Dr. Margaret Brennan. I taught English literature for thirty years." Her tone suggested she was still grading papers and finding them all inadequate. She glanced at Sam's notebook. "Finally, someone who takes this seriously."

Professor—sharp, Sam wrote, not sure whether to be pleased or worried that the intimidating professor approved of her methods.

A nervous-looking man in his early forties went next. "Gerald Parker. I'm the club treasurer." He cleared his throat. "Speaking of which, we really do need to collect dues."

Several people groaned.

Treasurer, Sam noted after Gerald's name.

A dark-haired woman in her thirties gave Sam a shy smile. "Sofia Smith. I'm a grad student at Western Carolina. I just joined a couple of months ago, so I'm almost as new as you." Sofia had dark eyes that seemed older than her years.

Grad student—friendly. At least Sam wasn't the only recent addition. And Sofia seemed slightly familiar. She wanted to say she worked at the coffee shop downtown.

"Dylan Morrison." The young man in his twenties had the deliberately unkempt look of someone who wanted to be taken seriously as an artist. "I write poetry." He said this with a slight challenge in his voice, eyes flicking to Dr. Brennan as if expecting criticism. Then he glanced curiously at Sam's notebook. He grinned. "Let me guess. You're going to write *the scruffy one*, aren't you?"

"What? No! I'm just jotting down notes to help me remember who's who." Sam pulled the notebook just a little closer to her, although no one could see what she was writing.

"She's organized," Olivia said, coming to her rescue. "It's her thing."

Next to Dylan's name, she wrote *poet—defensive*? She looked up to find Dylan still watching her with amusement. "I'm definitely getting an adjective," he muttered.

"We all are," Gerald, the treasurer, said dryly. "That's the point."

"Pamela Cross," said a woman in her late-fifties with a kind face. "Retired librarian. I love finding good book communities." She said it with such genuine warmth that Sam immediately liked her. "I think it's smart," she added, nodding at the notebook. "I wish I'd done that at my first meeting."

Librarian—sweet. Sam put a small star next to her name.

The last woman, early fifties with laugh lines and an easy manner, beamed at Sam. "I'm Claire Mills, the club president. We've emailed! I'm so glad you made it." She smiled at the notebook. "Don't worry. Half of us won't remember your name by next month anyway."

"I will," Gerald said. "You're 'notebook girl' now, Sam."

"Could be worse," Sam said, clicking her pen.

Beside Claire's name, Sam wrote *president—organized.* She could tell Claire actually read all her emails and responded right away.

"That's everyone," Charlotte said. "Let's get started. Gerald, maybe handle the dues by email this time?"

Gerald's mouth tightened, but he nodded.

"Or perhaps someone else could handle it?" Margaret, the professor, said lightly. "You seem to have so much on your plate these days. So many . . . projects."

Gerald's face went from pale to flushed. "I'll handle it.

Claire, the club president, took over with the practiced ease of someone used to wrangling strong personalities. "Tonight we're discussing *The Memory Keeper.* It's a literary mystery about a woman who inherits her grandmother's bookstore and discovers cryptic notes in the margins of old books. Did everyone finish the book?"

There were nods all around.

"Wonderful. Sam, this group actually reads the books, which makes us unusual." She smiled. "I'll start. I absolutely *loved* this book."

"It was dreadful," Margaret interrupted. "Predictable women's fiction tripe masquerading as literature. Maudlin sentimentality, amateur prose, and that tired bookstore-as-metaphor trope."

An awkward silence fell.

Charlotte laughed, breaking the tension. "Tell us what you *really* think, Margaret."

"That is all." The professor sniffed as she took a sip of her drink. Although everyone else seemed to be drinking the tea Charlotte had prepared, Margaret had a coffee mug. Sam had noticed Charlotte had a coffee pot in the other room. She apparently demanded special treatment.

"Okay!" said Claire brightly, casting a worried glance at Sam as if Margaret's little diatribe might run her off screaming from her first book club meeting. She gave a stressed, tinkling laugh. "Margaret usually takes the dissenting position. As she mentioned, she's a retired English professor, so she has rather strong opinions."

"Someone needs to maintain standards," Margaret said crisply.

Sam glanced around the room. Dylan, the young poet, was glaring at Margaret. Gerald, the treasurer, looked as if he wanted to sink through the floor. Retired librarian Pamela, was studying her book with intense concentration. Sofia, the grad student, had a tight jaw. Only Claire, the club president, seemed unruffled, although her smile had turned fixed.

This was going to be an interesting group.

"This book was just about as awful as last month's selection," grouched the professor.

Claire gave her a repressive look. "Now, now. Not everyone felt that way about *The Cardiac Protocol*." She smiled at Sam. "It was about a brilliant cardiologist who discovers that patients in her hospital's cardiac unit are dying. She was trying to learn if they were medical errors, a disturbing random trend, or murder. Of course, it ended up being murder, since it's a medical thriller, ha. I found this a really riveting read. It reminded me of Michael Crichton."

The young man, Dylan, looked confused. "It reminded you of *Jurassic Park*?"

The professor snorted in derision, and Dylan flushed. She said, "Crichton also wrote medical thrillers." Margaret drank her coffee. "Though the book's medical accuracy was acceptable. However, the protagonist should have been more careful about drug interactions, as I mentioned at last month's meeting. One wrong combination with heart medication and that's it." She made a slashing motion across her throat.

"Personal experience?" asked Dylan, sounding almost hopeful.

"I'm on three different cardiac medications," Margaret said matter-of-factly. "You learn what not to mix."

"Let's get back to this month's selection," said Claire, trying to get the meeting back on track.

Each of the members gave their opinions of *The Memory Keeper*. Everyone except Margaret was quite complimentary of the writing and the story's plot.

Sam said, "I thought it was a great read." She opened her copy of the book, which was littered with sticky notes and full of marginalia. "The fact I wrote so much in the margins is a sign I enjoyed it. But for me, there are different ways of enjoying a book. If I'm absorbed in it, for whatever reason, it's doing its job. Maybe it's that I just want to make sure that the bad guy gets punished. Maybe there's a subplot I'm interested in following. Regardless, it's transportive, isn't it? It takes us to another realm."

There were eager nods of heads at this. Even the professor gave a stiff bob of hers in acknowledgment.

Then there was a discussion time where they got more into the nitty-gritty of the book and various storylines. They sipped their tea and listened to the others. Following that, Claire said, "Okay, let's choose our pick for next month. There were a few books that were bandied around at the last meeting. One of them was that historical romance, *A Season in Florence*."

Margaret Brennan was dismissive. "Romance novels are hardly literature. We should challenge ourselves intellectually."

"Some of us are already doing that and could use a break," said Sofia quietly. Sam recalled her saying she was a grad student. She was probably buried in reading.

Margaret gave Sofia a cold look. Sofia raised her chin in an almost challenging posture.

Dylan said slowly, "There's a new poetry collection by Ocean Vuong."

The professor said, "Poetry requires sharp group discussion to work. I suggest *Middlemarch*. A true classic many people claim to read but haven't."

Sofia cleared her throat. "That's quite long, I think. Maybe we should choose something more accessible?"

"Accessible is another word for unchallenging," said the professor sharply.

There was a brief pause before Pamela, the retired librarian, said, "What about *Remains of the Day* by Kazuo Ishiguro? That's literary but with a manageable length."

Gerald, who'd been pestering everyone about their dues, checked his notes in a small notebook he'd brought in. "We read that two years ago."

"Then we'll read *Middlemarch*. Unless anyone has serious objections?" Margaret said this in a tone that discouraged objections.

They all agreed. With the next month's selection chosen, they adjourned to chat and have more tea. Charlotte busied herself at the cash register, checking out the few copies of the book that she had in stock and promising to order the rest for everyone later.

"What did you make of your first meeting?" asked Olivia in an undertone as they stood in a corner of the bookstore.

Sam cast a look behind her to make sure Margaret was out of earshot and saw the professor was still sitting in the back room of the bookshop, drinking her coffee. "It was good. I liked the book. And it seems like a really good group. Although one member showed up in a cranky mood."

"Margaret?" Olivia snorted. "She's always like that. Sorry if it was off-putting."

"No, it's fine. It probably helps with discussion, right? Having a dissenting voice."

Olivia said wryly, "I could handle it easier if she weren't *quite* so dissenting. Anyway, I'm glad you came. It's been good for me to get out of the house. Of course, my volunteering gets me out, too. It's just so quiet there, and I feel like I'm rattling around."

Olivia was a widow, and her younger brother, Jason, had moved out fairly recently after getting a job. Her house was a big one, and Sam knew exactly how she felt since she was alone in a large house, too. "You don't want to move out?" They started walking out the exit of the bookshop, giving Charlotte a wave as they left.

"I just don't want the trouble, you know? That's more work than I feel like I'm up to right now. Plus, I think it would be really emotional. On top of it all, I love living in Maple Hills. Our neighbors are great. If I move to another subdivision, I won't really know what I'm going to get."

Sam nodded. "Makes sense. That's also why I'm staying put. Having Arlo really helps, too."

"Actually, speaking of Arlo, I have something to tell you. I've been thinking about what you said before about getting a pet. I filled out an application at the shelter last week."

Sam said, "Seriously? That's great!"

"There's this older cat there that I really loved when I was walking around. She's nine, which apparently makes her tough to adopt. She's got these beautiful green eyes. When I sat with her, she just curled up in my lap and started purring like a little motor. She acted so relieved and happy that I was there. The shelter volunteer said she'd never seen her do that with anyone before."

Sam said softly, "She chose you."

"That's what it felt like. The shelter said they'd call me this week to finalize everything."

Sam said, "She sounds perfect for you, Olivia."

They chatted for a few more minutes, then Olivia gave her a quick hug, and they went their separate ways. Minutes later, Sam was opening her front door as Arlo greeted her enthusiastically.

"Hey boy," crooned Sam. "Did you miss me? I wasn't gone that long."

Arlo apparently disagreed with this assessment. He ran in excited circles for a few seconds before leaping up on the sofa to join Sam as she grabbed the selection for the following month and her reading supplies.

Sam took a look at *Middlemarch* by George Eliot. All 880 pages of it. She had her purple gel pen (best for marginalia), a pack of color-coded sticky tabs, and index cards. She labeled three of the cards *characters*, *themes*, and *discussion questions*.

Arlo watched this setup with what might have been judgment.

"Don't look at me like that, buddy," Sam told him. "Margaret specifically picked this book to intimidate people. I'm not showing up unprepared."

She opened to the first page, clicked her pen, and began reading. By page ten, she had two yellow tabs (beautiful prose), one blue tab (key theme), and had started a character list on her index card.

"This is going to be a long month," she murmured to Arlo, who'd already fallen asleep.

Sam kept reading.

Chapter Two

The next morning, Sam woke up early. Arlo, still bleary-eyed, lay on her feet, yawning.

"I need my feet back so I can get out of the bed," she advised the dog.

Arlo allowed her to have them back, continuing to yawn as Sam climbed out of the bed.

An hour and a half later, Sam had exercised, walked Arlo, showered, dressed, and eaten. This was Sam's usual routine. The only thing Sam found consistently challenging was relaxing. It was so hard to relax that she had to put it on her planner as a task to complete. But she was working on getting better at it.

The phone rang right before eight o'clock. Glancing down at the screen, she saw it was Charlotte.

"Good morning," she said. "What did you make of the meeting last night? I hope Margaret didn't scare you away. But I think you're made of sterner stuff."

Sam smiled. "She didn't. Olivia asked me the same thing. I told Olivia that having someone like Margaret around makes for interesting discussions."

"Oh good. I was kind of wincing during the whole thing. I'm used to the professor, but I was thinking of how she sounded to a newcomer."

Sam said, "I bet she was tough in the classroom."

"Yeah. I'm very glad I wasn't her student. And I love English literature! Anyway, I wanted to ask you if you were busy today. You mentioned last week that you might be able to help me out with changing up my social media for the bookstore."

"Oh, right," said Sam. "Yes, you wanted it to be more brand-ed, didn't you? I'm totally free. Do you want to meet up now, or do you have things to do at the store first thing?"

"Actually, it would work out great if you're free now. I've got a truck of books coming in later today that's going to mean some work later on. Are you sure right now is okay? I can meet you at the store. I'm getting ready to head over there in just a minute."

Sam said, "Sure. I'll be right there."

She gave Arlo a quick rub. He had gone straight from her bedroom to the sofa, foregoing watching Sam exercise, eat, or getting ready. He opened a lazy eye in acknowledgment before letting it close again. A second later, he was snoring.

Twice-Told Tales was a Victorian building on Main Street, its brick façade painted a warm cream with hunter green around the tall windows. The shop had sustained damage during a hurricane that had hit the town recently, so it sported a new roof. A hand-painted wooden sign hung from a wrought-iron bracket above the door.

Charlotte was just unlocking the door. She smiled at Sam. "Thanks again for doing this. I'm hopeless when it comes to so-cial media and that design app."

"That's not true. You've done a great job keeping up with an online presence."

Charlotte said ruefully, "Yeah, but it's not obvious it's coming from my shop. And I don't feel like I'm consistent in the kinds of things I post. In other words, I need a plan. And you're the best person I know for planning things."

"I think I take it into the realm of obsessive," said Sam with a laugh. "Anyway, I'm happy to help out. Let's fire up your computer and we'll get you started on Canva. It does a fantastic job with design."

"Okay. Let's head into the back room. I can put my laptop on one of the tables in there so we can both look at it. Do you want some coffee? I think I'll make a pot."

"Sure."

They chatted for a few minutes while Charlotte started the coffeemaker and the java perked. Then Charlotte got a couple of cups and, after doctoring their coffee with cream and sugar, they headed for the back room.

Which was where they stopped short. Margaret Brennan was slumped in a chair, cup of coffee beside her. Dead.

Chapter Three

Charlotte gave a cry of dismay as Sam rushed forward to look for a pulse. Finding none, she said, "Charlotte, you'll need to call the police."

Charlotte, white-faced, gave a quick bob of her head as she fumbled to get her phone out of her pocket.

Sam stepped away from the professor's body, her gaze scanning the scene. When she'd checked for a pulse, she had seen no signs of trauma on Margaret. And she hadn't seen marks from a ligature around her throat. Had Margaret suffered a heart attack or stroke? She wasn't a young woman. Sam looked again at the coffee cup next to Margaret. Had someone tampered with her drink last night?

"They're on their way," said Charlotte, sounding a little breathless.

"Let's move outside the building," said Sam. "The police may want us out of here."

Charlotte silently nodded as they walked toward the exit. She turned the sign to 'closed' as they left.

Sam gave her friend a quick hug. "Hey, are you okay?"

"Not really," said Charlotte in a trembling voice. "Margaret must have been in there all night, Sam. I just feel sick over it."

"You didn't know she was there. You must have assumed everyone had left when you locked up."

Charlotte took a steadying breath. "For sure. I was just busy checking folks out at the register and straightening up before I left the building."

"And you didn't check the back room again. Why would you?"

Charlotte said, "That's right. The light switch for that room is in the main room. Everyone is always really good about cleaning up after themselves, so I figured I'd just tidy the room this morning, if it even needed it at all." She said in a whisper, "I never dreamed Margaret would still be in there. Do you think she had a heart attack? Could she have been dying in there while the rest of us were in the other room?" Charlotte had a horrified expression on her face.

"I'm not sure. But the police will get to the bottom of it."

A sedan drove to the front of the store. The police chief, Harold Hawkins, quickly got out. He was in his late-fifties, with a stocky build.

"Ms. Prescott. Of course you're here," he said.

Sam had the feeling Chief Hawkins thought she had an uncanny ability to be around when crimes occurred. It was a trait that didn't appear to endear her to him, although she thought they'd reached something of a detente during the last investigation she was part of. "Chief Hawkins," she said.

Charlotte said, "She's in the back room of the store."

They watched silently as he swiftly strode into Twice-Told Tales. A few minutes later, he came back outside, wearing a grim expression. He reached into his car, pulling out crime scene tape. Charlotte looked even more worried than she had before as he strung it up outside her store.

After securing the scene, the chief stepped away to make a couple of phone calls. Then he joined them again, eyes serious. "Do you know who the woman is?"

Charlotte nodded miserably. "It's Dr. Margaret Brennan. She's a retired professor."

Hawkins had taken out a small notebook and pencil. He carefully jotted this information down before asking, "And how long as she been in the shop?"

Charlotte took another deep breath. "Overnight."

Hawkins raised his eyebrows at this as he made a note of this. "Can you explain that a little further?"

That was when Charlotte burst into tears. Sam reached into her purse and pulled out a packet of tissues, gently putting it into her friend's hand.

The chief was now looking at Sam somewhat impatiently. Sam said, "Charlotte hosted the monthly book club meeting in the shop's back room last night. The professor was one of the members. Obviously, we all thought she'd left, but she hadn't. Charlotte locked up and went home without realizing anyone was still in the store."

Another police car pulled up, and Officer Martinez, an officer in her early 30s wearing a crisp uniform, joined them. The chief looked glad to see her. He said, "Martinez, could you speak with Charlotte Webb? Maybe get her a cup of coffee from the shop down the street? Actually, if the shop is quiet enough, that might be a better place to get a statement."

Martinez gently took Charlotte by the arm and led her off, still quietly sobbing, toward the coffeehouse.

Hawkins turned back toward Sam. "Okay, give me a rundown of what happened last night."

Sam cleared her throat. "I'm guessing this is a suspicious death."

"Until we know otherwise, I'm treating it that way. The medical examiner and the crime scene techs are on their way. I'll need to contact the state police, too. Now, the rundown?"

Sam said slowly, "It was my first time at the book club, so everything was new to me."

Hawkins gave her a wry look. "I have the feeling you went home and took notes."

Sam didn't answer this because it was true, and she didn't want to become a cliché. "Charlotte hosts the club in the back room of the store. We had tea to kind of set the vibe coming in. Except for Margaret Brennan."

"What did she drink?" asked the chief.

"Coffee."

"This was at night, though?" Hawkins frowned.

"That's right. Seven-thirty. Maybe Margaret was used to consuming caffeine at night. Anyway, she had a different drink from everyone else, so it would definitely have been easy to identify it, if someone was wanting to poison her."

Hawkins raised his eyebrows. "You seem pretty positive about that poison."

"It's just a guess. She could have had some sort of major medical event, of course. I'm just covering the bases."

"What makes you think it could have been a homicide?" asked Hawkins.

Sam said slowly, "There seemed like there was a lot of tension between Margaret and the other club members. A lot of pent-up hostility."

"That's a pretty strong statement."

Sam nodded. "But it's true. I'd never met Margaret before last night, but I could tell she was the kind of person who didn't hold back. She said exactly what was on her mind with no regard for anybody's feelings."

"Whose feelings did you think she might have hurt? And give me an overview of the people who attended last night, in the process."

Fortunately, Sam *had* taken those notes that Hawkins had been so derisive about. So she could easily recite who was there. Sometimes, being Type-A was useful.

"Claire Mills is the club president. She's very chipper and eager to expand the club. Gerald Parker was there; he's the treasurer. Sofia Smith, a grad student. Dylan Morrison, a poet. And a retired librarian named Pamela Cross."

"No one else?"

Sam said, "Well, Olivia was there. And Charlotte."

Hawkins said, "Olivia Stanton?"

"That's right." Sam was reluctant to even confirm Olivia's presence there. She'd been a suspect before and it didn't seem quite fair for her to be one again.

Hawkins was carefully making notes as Sam named the members. Giving a bob of his head, he said, "And you felt that tension coming from everybody?"

"That's right. The air was thick with it. I thought maybe it was because I was there as a new member and everyone wanted to make a good impression."

"But Margaret Brennan was less concerned about that?" asked Hawkins.

"Correct. She slammed the book they'd read. And she argued over the next selection the club was choosing."

Hawkins nodded. "What was her manner like when she was doing this? In other words, was she just straightforward with her criticism and other statements?"

"Honestly, it seemed more mean-spirited. I can't imagine how she must have been in the classroom."

Hawkins raised his eyebrows. "She taught kids?"

"College students. But I bet she must have cowed everybody in her classroom. Anyway, the point was that she seemed like a tough, straight-shooting person. That doesn't mean she was murdered, of course. It just means that I wouldn't be shocked to discover she'd gotten on someone's bad side."

Hawkins nodded. "Okay. Did you actually see anyone tampering with her coffee cup?"

"No. But I wasn't expecting her to die, of course. In general, it was the kind of environment where someone *could* have easily tampered with her cup. There was lots of milling around and chit-chatting before Charlotte called the meeting to order."

Hawkins said, "Tell me what happened following the meeting."

Sam shrugged. "We adjourned. People were paying Charlotte for the next month's selection. We put our folding chairs away and brought our teacups in the main room of the bookshop. People were still talking with each other when Olivia and I walked out together."

"And no one noticed Margaret Brennan was left behind?"

Sam said, "No. Charlotte said she assumed everyone had left by the time she was closing up the shop."

"It seems like she'd have noticed her in there when she was turning off the lights for the night."

Sam shook her head. "No. The light switch for that room is on the wall leading into it. It's in the main bookshop area."

"Okay." Hawkins made another note, then tapped his pencil on the notepad. "I may need to get in touch with you again for more information."

"Not a problem." Sam looked down the street and saw a much calmer-looking Charlotte leaving the coffeehouse with Martinez in tow.

Charlotte walked up to Sam as Martinez and Hawkins went into the shop. "I don't even know what to say about all this."

"It sounds like you won't have your shop back for a while. Would you like to come over to my house? Or do you feel more like resting at your own?"

Charlotte considered this before saying slowly, "You know, I think I want to talk this over a little bit. That might be better than me running it all through my head by myself. Do you mind?"

"Are you kidding? I live to entertain," said Sam, totally truthfully. "Would you like me to drive you? I can drive you back later to get your car."

"No, I'm good to drive. I'll meet you at your place."

Chapter Four

A few minutes later, Sam and Charlotte were walking into Sam's house. Sam said, "Have a seat anywhere. Would you like coffee, tea, something stronger?"

Charlotte gave a small laugh. "I think if I have something stronger then I'd fall asleep. I'll stick with a coffee."

Sam joined Charlotte a few minutes later with a tray holding two coffees, cream, sugar, and muffins.

Charlotte gave her a wry look. "I'd never know you just found a body unless I'd been right there with you."

"Yes, but the body wasn't in my bookshop. That must have been a really awful jolt for you. And you knew Margaret well, too. I didn't."

Charlotte added a lot of cream and sugar to her coffee cup. "I feel horrible that it happened. I'm just not even sure what to think. Did she have a heart attack or something? I really hope it was a natural death. Not that I wanted Margaret to die for *any* reason, but it would be so much worse if she was murdered."

"Do you think she might have been?" asked Sam quietly.

Charlotte was quiet as she took a couple of sips of her coffee. "I'm not sure. I hate to even think somebody I know is a killer. I really do. I mean, I'm with those folks at least once a month. I've gotten to know them to the point where they feel like friends instead of just customers. It's pretty hard to imagine any of them could do something like that."

Sam said, "When I was at the meeting last night, I didn't get the best impression of Margaret. I'm not sure if she was having a really off night or if she was always like that." She remembered Olivia saying that was normal for Margaret, but wanted to hear Charlotte's opinion, too.

"Unfortunately, that was typical behavior for Margaret. She was a tough woman. She must have been a nightmare in the classroom." Charlotte paused, sighing. "She spent thirty years teaching English literature. Maybe it was natural for her to take a dissenting position in every discussion. But she could be a very harsh critic and not just on the books we were reading. The book club members came under the gun, too. She made several members uncomfortable over time."

Sam said, "Was there ever a point where you felt you needed to talk to her about that? Ask her to tone it down?"

"Sure. A couple of times I gently brought it up, privately. But Margaret didn't listen."

Sam asked, "Did you ever consider asking her to leave the club?"

"No. We all talked about that one week when Margaret didn't attend. We decided she could be difficult, but everyone tolerated her because she did contribute to the discussions. Recently, though, there has been more tension than usual in the club."

"With anyone in particular?" asked Sam.

Charlotte gave a short laugh. "With just about everybody. For example, Margaret gave a scathing critique of Claire's manuscript."

"Her manuscript? I didn't know Claire was a writer." She knew the club president seemed to be a very organized person. That might translate well over into writing.

Charlotte said, "Claire wrote a romance. She'd been working and reworking the story for years, trying to get every word just the way she wanted it. And Margaret tore it apart."

"I'm surprised Claire would want Margaret to read it at all. She must have known it wasn't Margaret's usual genre to read. Plus, Margaret seemed like a really critical person."

Charlotte nodded. "I know. But Claire was at the point where she'd revised the book so much, she didn't have any perspective on it anymore. She thought Margaret could look at it with fresh eyes. But it wasn't ideal. Margaret always sneers about genre fiction, especially romance. I was worried about it from the very start. I had the feeling Claire thought she could handle feedback better than she actually could. After all, that book was almost like her baby. She'd been working on it for ages."

"That must have been devastating for Claire, especially after all the hard work she put into writing the book. Did anybody else cross Margaret lately?"

Charlotte considered this. "Dylan had a really disastrous open mic night at the coffeehouse. Margaret played a big part in that."

"He was reading his poetry?"

"That's right," said Charlotte. She set down her cup. "He was really upset. Dylan seems pretty sensitive to me. I kept telling both him and Claire to take no notice of Margaret. Both of them were really hurt. And the others have been nervous or uncomfortable around Margaret lately, so there might have been other issues that I don't know about. She had a way of ferreting out information on others. Like she enjoyed finding weak spots."

"Do you think she was bored and that's why she was acting that way? I know Margaret was retired. Or was that simply her personality?"

Charlotte said, "Both. She definitely had a difficult personality. But she probably missed the classroom in some ways. After all, she was in charge there. She was the kind of person who liked being in control." She set down her coffee cup. "Hey, thanks for this, Sam. I feel a lot better now, which is probably a combination of the coffee, talking it out, and Arlo."

Arlo gave her a fetching doggy grin and nuzzled her hand. "You'll have to come by the shop," Charlotte said to the little dog. "I have a jar of dog treats there for my canine visitors." She stood. "I'm going to get out of your hair now. I think I'll go home and do some housework. I still feel sort of restless, so that might be good for me."

Sam and Arlo walked her to the door. "Let me know if you need anything later," Sam said. "I'm always here if you need an ear."

Charlotte gave her a hug and Arlo a rub before she headed out the door to her car.

The mention of housework made Sam decide to do some of her own. She felt just as restless as Charlotte, and cleaning up was traditionally the best way for her to handle it.

She was just tidying up her linen closet when the phone rang. It was Aiden. "Hey there. I heard what happened. Are you okay?"

Sam felt her heart lift at the sound of Aiden's voice. They were in that gray area where they were seeing a fair amount of each other, but hadn't labeled their status. He was a former police officer turned teacher, so she wasn't surprised that he'd heard the news about Margaret's death. He still had a lot of friends on the local force.

"I'm okay, thanks. I feel bad for poor Charlotte, though. Aren't you at school?"

"I am, but I'm on my planning period right now. I can spare a few minutes. So you and Charlotte were the ones to discover her?" he asked.

"That's right. I'd only just met Margaret last night at the book club meeting, but Charlotte knew her for a while. And, of course, she died at Charlotte's shop, which also makes it especially tough."

Aiden said, "I'd forgotten you started book club last night."

"Did your source at the police station mention how Margaret died?"

Aiden said, "Only that they were treating it as a suspicious death until they knew otherwise. But forensics will have to confirm whether it was a natural event or not. I understand Margaret didn't have many friends in the group."

"Unfortunately not. But then, Margaret kind of did that to herself, from what I heard. She was very opinionated and not worried about sharing what was on her mind. A real straight-shooter."

Aiden said, "And you're planning on looking into Margaret's death."

"I wouldn't say I'm looking *into* it. But I do feel personally invested, considering I was with Charlotte when Margaret was found. I might do some digging. I'll keep the police informed, of course." Sam paused. "And I'd love to have you help me out."

"You know I will," said Aiden, sounding rueful. "Listen, I've got to run for now. I'll check back in with you later. Please be careful."

Chapter Five

It was a bit later when Sam heard the doorbell ring. She peeked out the side window before opening the door to Claire Brennan, the book club president.

Claire started out apologetically before Sam could say anything. "Hey there. I'm so sorry about dropping by like this. I didn't have your phone number, so I just looked up your address online."

"No, you're fine. Come on inside. Coffee? Tea?" Sam automatically fell into hostess mode, even with a surprise guest.

"Actually, if you've already got coffee made, I'd love a cup. But don't make a pot just for me."

Sam smiled at her. "It's already made. I needed an extra energy boost today."

Arlo greeted Claire with a tail wag and an earnest expression on his face.

"And who is this cutie?" asked Claire, stooping down to rub Arlo. Arlo immediately flopped over on his back for a belly rub.

"Arlo. He's clearly taken to you." Sam walked into the kitchen to pull out the tray again and load it with a second round of coffees and muffins.

They settled in the sunroom. Arlo leaned up against Claire's legs as she doctored her coffee. Claire said, "I'm sure you're wondering why I'm here."

"You've heard about what happened at the bookstore this morning, haven't you?"

Claire said, "I heard *something* happened at the bookstore. Someone posted a picture on social media with crime scene tape and police cars all over the place. I did hear you and Charlotte were there. I tried calling Charlotte, but her phone is turned off. Is she okay?"

"She's fine. Just overwhelmed, I think." Sam paused. The police hadn't told her to keep the information under her hat, but it seemed as if Margaret's family should be notified before anyone else knew about her death. "Before I say anything, do you know if Margaret has any family here in town? A husband?"

Claire shook her head. "No husband. And she doesn't have anyone at all in town, from what I understand. She'd said once, a while back, that she had a child she was estranged from. Sadly, it didn't come as a huge surprise, knowing how Margaret is." She paused, frowning. "Wait, did something happen to Margaret?"

"I'm afraid so. When Charlotte and I walked into her shop this morning, we found Margaret there. She was dead."

Sam watched Claire's reaction carefully. She saw shock pass over her features before something she thought might be relief replaced it. "I can't believe it," Claire breathed. "How did she get in there? Did Margaret break into Twice-Told Tales? Why would she do something like that?"

"It looked like she'd been in the shop all night. That she'd never left."

Claire's eyes widened. "You mean she died in that back room before we walked out of the bookshop."

"The police haven't said when she died. But at some point following the end of the meeting, yes."

Claire was silent for a couple of moments, just petting Arlo. "So did she have some kind of medical emergency? But she couldn't call out to us?"

"The police have to treat it like a suspicious death until they know more," said Sam carefully.

Claire shook her head. "You mean somebody might have killed her somehow? What, strangled her?"

"That's something the police are looking into," said Sam.

"I just can't believe it. I mean, a lot of folks had their issues with Margaret, but I don't see anybody in our book club as a killer." She gave a short laugh. "I can't even believe I'm saying those words. Of *course* no one in our book club is a killer. Margaret must have had a stroke or something. She wasn't the healthiest person out there, or the youngest."

"Maybe that's what the police will learn after the autopsy."

Claire said, "Hey, I'm so sorry about all this. You thought you were joining a harmless little book club. And you've stepped into a real hornet's nest."

"It's not anybody's fault. The group seems great. I did notice some tension among the members and Margaret."

Claire sighed. "Yeah, I guess that's totally obvious. Margaret, bless her, could be a tough person to get along with. But she always had a different take on the book discussions." She shook her head wryly. "We might have all loved a story, but Margaret would find something horribly wrong with it."

"What did everybody make of that?"

Claire said, "At first, I think we all took it personally. But the point of art is what it makes you feel, right? And to pay attention to that, whether it's a painting or a book. It's okay not to like something. Eventually, we got used to Margaret filling the role of the devil's advocate. Honestly, she added a lot to the book discussions. It would have been a pretty boring club if all of us loved every book and didn't have much to say about it."

"Did anyone seem to have anything against Margaret personally? Like I said, it did sometimes seem tense in the group last night."

Claire rubbed her face as if she were exhausted. "Not to the degree that someone would decide to take her life, no. Of course not. But we probably all had our beefs with Margaret." She hesitated. "I did, too. I've been working on writing a romance for, oh, what feels like most of my life."

"Really? That's amazing."

Claire gave Sam a rueful look. "Is it? It feels like such a slog right now. And every time I think I'm done with it, I keep fiddling with the plot or the characters. Or I'll read an article online about a cool writing technique and try to add it to the story. I've probably edited all the life out of it at this point. Anyway, I was stupid enough to give it to Margaret to read."

"That took a lot of courage."

"You're not kidding," said Claire. "I must have been out of my mind. But then, in some ways it makes sense. Margaret was a literature professor for her entire career. She was an expert at ferreting out what's wrong with a book or a paper and telling you how to fix it. I thought that might be the best way to get an objective opinion on my story. Because, by that time, I'd totally lost my perspective on the book. I didn't know if it was good or bad anymore."

"I'm guessing sharing it with Margaret didn't go well?" asked Sam.

Claire gave a short laugh. "It did not. She ripped it to shreds. But then, I'd basically asked for it. The last thing I wanted was to give it to someone like my mom, who'd tell me it was absolutely perfect. That would have been useless feedback."

Claire sounded as if she'd handled the critique very well. But Sam could see stress lines appearing at the corners of her eyes and mouth. She wondered if it had been as easy to accept the feedback as Claire made it sound.

Claire continued, "I wasn't the only one Margaret hurt, of course. I don't even know what happened between Gerald and Margaret. He's been acting so strange lately."

"Really?"

"Yeah. Just very nervous and jumpy. Agitated, I guess you'd say. He barely said a word at the meeting and that's not like him," said Claire. Then she frowned. "But I love Gerald. I'm not saying he had anything to do with whatever happened to Margaret. I think everybody in the book club has probably run afoul of her at some point. It makes me wince whenever we have a new member. Margaret did make things uncomfortable sometimes. I figured you'd pick up on that." She gave Sam a small smile. "Are we going to be able to tempt you to come back?"

"Absolutely. I've already started reading *Middlemarch* for next month and am making notes."

"Perfect," said Claire. She gave Arlo one last rub, then stood up. "I should be heading out. Thanks for filling me in. If you do happen to hear anything else, please feel free to let me know. As president of the book club, I should know what's happening."

"Of course I will," said Sam.

After Claire left, Sam said to Arlo, "Maybe you and I need to have a walk."

Arlo's ears pricked up, and he gave Sam a doggy grin before making a quick run in a circle. She laughed. "Okay, you think so, too. We need to stretch our legs. And maybe I need some air while I process everything."

Arlo gave joyful leaps as Sam got his leash and harness out of the coat closet. They headed outside, sunshine beaming through the trees. They'd barely made it past the third house when Nora emerged from her front door. Nora was Sam's elderly neighbor. She kept the entire neighborhood on its toes. And somehow, she managed to know just about everything that was going on.

"Here we go," said Sam in an undertone to Arlo. Arlo wagged his tail in agreement, although he really liked Nora. But then, his relationship with Nora was less complicated.

The old woman strode up to them. "Good morning, Sam. I saw you had a visitor early this morning. Wasn't it Claire Mills?"

Sam smiled at Nora. "You're right. She was coming by for a brief visit. I've joined her book club at Twice-Told Tales." Sam had no intention of sharing anything else with Nora, who would take it and run with the information. That was how the entire town of Sunset Ridge would find out.

But Sam should have known that Nora was already aware of what had happened. She said, "I heard what happened at the bookstore this morning." Her mouth twisted down in a frown. "Horrible. I don't know what the world is coming to. Margaret Brennan, of all people."

So word had somehow apparently gotten out.

"She might have passed from natural causes."

But Nora was already shaking her head. "It seems unlikely, doesn't it?"

"How on earth did you find out about this, Nora?"

Nora looked pleased with herself. "After the hurricane, I decided I needed more ways to find out what's going on in town. I bought a police scanner. It's been endlessly entertaining. At any rate, it was terribly tragic. Awful." She waited a few moments before saying, "Though I can't say I'm entirely surprised."

"Oh?"

"That's right. Margaret Brennan was not a well-liked woman. She never seemed to *want* to be a well-liked woman. She couldn't seem to keep herself from injecting her opinion into everything. I saw her at the grocery store one time, telling some poor woman why she'd just chosen the wrong pasta sauce."

Sam gave a small smile. "A woman who knew her own mind."

Nora waved her hand in the air. "And what good does that do you when nobody wants to spend time with you?"

"Do you think Margaret was lonely?"

Nora shrugged. "She'd driven everyone away. She didn't have any friends. She *had* to have been lonely. But she couldn't stop herself. She offered her opinion whether anyone wanted to hear it or not." She gave Sam a summing-up look. "This book club you went to. Was it last night, then? Was Margaret there?"

Sam tried to deflect the question. "What makes you think she was?"

Nora rolled her eyes. "It's obvious, isn't it? The police were over at Twice-Told Tales right after the shop opened for the day. Margaret was found dead in there. It seems she must have been in the store overnight."

Sam said slowly, "Yes, the club meeting was last night. I don't really know anything about what happened. Actually, you probably know more than I do, considering you're listening to your scanner."

"Hmph. If you say so." Nora paused. "I went to that book club a few times, myself."

"You're not still a member?"

"Nope," said Nora. "The books really weren't for me. Not the kind of stuff I like to read. I remember some of the members there, though. Gerald was one of them. I don't really remember his last name."

"Parker."

Nora's eyes narrowed. "You and your excellent memory."

"Me and my excellent notes. That's how I learn."

"Whatever. Anyway, I saw him at the bank the other day. I told him he looked absolutely miserable."

Sam hid a smile. "Wow. He must have really appreciated that."

"He should have. Maybe that was a reminder to him that he needed to smile at his customers more."

Sam asked, "What does Gerald do at the bank?"

"He's a teller. But the man really does seem to have something on his mind. Was he that bad at book club last night?"

"Not really," said Sam. "Of course, I don't know him well. He was focused on getting the dues paid. If he's a bank teller, it makes sense he's the club treasurer."

"I'm not sure why you even need dues for a book club."

Sam said, "From what I gather, they sometimes have special meetings where supper is served. And I think there's a party or two during the year."

Arlo gave a little tug at his leash, and Sam reached down to rub him. She was ready to keep walking, too. She changed the subject to something Nora rarely liked talking about. Dating. That might wrap up the conversation more quickly than a mysterious death at a bookshop. "Say, how's everything going with you? Any news on the dating front?"

Nora scowled. "It's terrible out there, Sam. I advise you jumpstart your relationship with Aiden. You wouldn't want to try to find someone else." She peered at Sam. "You're still in the friend zone, aren't you?"

"Perhaps. What happened with your date?"

"You wouldn't believe it," said Nora. "This one listed himself as an adventurous foodie and an excellent conversationalist."

"He sounds like a good pick."

"He *sounded* that way. But then he showed up twenty minutes late, wearing a fanny pack. Not one of those new, trendy ones, mind you. A beige number, circa 1987."

Sam tried to look sympathetic while Arlo sniffed a particularly interesting bush.

"The second red flag happened when he spent the entire appetizer course explaining his cryptocurrency investment strategy. In detail. I don't even know what a blockchain is. After forty minutes of explanation, I still don't."

Sam said, "That sounds pretty bad, I have to admit."

"And here's the kicker. When the entrees arrived, he pulled out a Tupperware container from the fanny pack."

"He didn't," said Sam, genuinely curious now, despite herself.

"He did! He said restaurant portions were 'financially irresponsible' and he always brings containers to maximize value. Then he asked our waiter, the poor waiter Sam, to split his entrée in half so he could pack up his lunch for tomorrow."

Sam could only shake her head. "I'm sorry," she said again.

"I excused myself to the powder room and seriously considered climbing out the window. But I'm not as flexible as I used to be, and it was a second-floor bathroom."

Arlo looked up at Nora with what appeared to be sympathy.

Nora gave a barking laugh. "Even Arlo feels bad for me. Maybe I should just get a dog."

Sam bit back a smile. "What happened when you got back to the table? I'm assuming you *did* go back to the table."

"Oh, he was explaining to the couple seated at the next table why they should also be bringing Tupperware to restaurants. They looked terrified. I told myself I had a sudden migraine and left."

"Was he upset?"

Nora snorted. "Absolutely not. The man apparently can't pick up on subtext at all. He asked me when we could meet up next time. As if! There is no next time, Simon with the fanny pack!"

"Understandably," said Sam.

Nora's eyes narrowed thoughtfully. "I suppose you're doing your thing, aren't you?"

"What thing is that?"

"Investigating," said Nora. "I see that gleam in your eye. Just like Nancy Drew."

"I'm a bit older than Nancy. And no, I'm not *investigating*, per se. I'm just poking around. I leave investigating to the professionals."

Nora tilted her head to one side. "If you say so. The evidence suggests otherwise. Are you planning on talking to Gerald-the-bank-teller? Using the excuse of a financial transaction?"

Sam was about to refute this when she stopped. "Actually, I do have a check that came in."

"Well then."

Sam said, "But I ordinarily deposit checks through the app."

"Pardon?" Nora frowned.

"The bank has a phone application I can use to deposit checks."

Nora was shaking her head before Sam had even finished speaking. "I wouldn't trust that, Sam. I like a physical bank and actual people handling the check. Plus, it gives you the perfect time to talk to Gerald about whether he killed Margaret Brennan or not."

Sam gave Nora a wry look. "I don't think pressing somebody about a murder at their work place is a great idea."

Nora shrugged. "It's not as if he can escape the questioning. It sounds practically perfect to me." She considered it a bit more.

"Although you could catch him during his lunch break. It could be a natural meetup that way."

"Natural? With me stalking the man to the deli?"

Nora said, "No deli for Gerald Parker. He prefers bringing a brown bag lunch from home. He sits right outside the bank on a bench with a book every day. I toot my horn at him when I go by."

Probably terrifying the poor man in the process. "I don't know when his lunch break is."

"Sure you do," said Nora impatiently. "The bank closes every day between one and two. For heaven's sake, Sam. Surely, you must realize that."

"No. Because I do all my banking on the app."

Nora's tone was severe. "You must stop that right away. Go to the bank fifteen minutes before they reopen at two. Speak with Gerald, then cash your check. Problem solved."

Sam hadn't thought it was a problem. But Nora was so pleased with herself that she immediately agreed to the scheme before finally breaking away from her neighbor with a cheery wave and taking an eager Arlo on the remainder of his walk.

Chapter Six

After taking Arlo back home, Sam headed to her car to speak with Gerald. Her house was near the front entrance to the subdivision, but she took the long way to drive through Maple Hills. Sometimes, catching people who were out doing yardwork or walking their dogs was the best way for her to see her neighbors. Since she was the homeowner association president, she liked being able to touch base with as many people as she could and make sure there weren't any problems.

As she rounded the corner onto Cedar Lane, she spotted Alfred up on a ladder, adjusting something on his porch overhang. His new roof gleamed in the afternoon sun. There was no more blue tarp, as there had been months ago after an errant hurricane had detoured through the mountains. Mandy stood at the base of the ladder, one hand steadying it.

Sam pulled over and rolled down her window. "Looking good!"

Alfred glanced down, then carefully descended. "Not bad for an old guy, right?"

Mandy swatted his arm. "She means the roof."

"The roof too," Alfred said with a grin.

"It really does look good. The tarp is finally gone."

Mandy said, "Thank goodness for that." She came closer to Sam's car, lowering her voice conspiratorially. "Between you and me, I was starting to think the tarp was permanent."

"She wanted to paint it to match the house," Alfred said.

"I did not!"

Sam laughed. "Well, glad it all worked out. Good seeing you both. I'm on my way to the bank now, but let's catch up soon."

The Mountain Trust Bank occupied a historic brick building on Main Street. According to a small sign in the front, it was built in the 1920s during Sunset Ridge's early prosperity. It had a red brick façade with limestone trim and Art déco details around the entrance. There was a small parking lot on the side.

And, sure enough, Gerald Parker was seated quietly on a stone bench, reading a tremendous book that surely must be the book club selection. He had the slightly rumpled look of someone who's been fighting a losing battle with stress. Gerald wore a very bank-appropriate outfit of a white shirt (somewhat wrinkled), conservative tie, and khaki pants.

"How's *Middlemarch*?" asked Sam lightly as she walked up.

Gerald put his hand up to shield his eyes from the sun as he glanced up from the story. His immediate reaction was one of suspicion, but it eased as he recognized Sam. "I'm liking it so far. George Eliot really knows how to write characters. I'm sixty pages in. Have you started reading it?"

"I'm on page 214," Sam admitted. "I had trouble sleeping last night, so I read instead."

Gerald's eyebrows shot up. "You're kidding. Book club, like, just happened."

Sam felt her cheeks warm slightly. "I know. It's a long book, so I wanted to get a head start."

"A head start," Gerald repeated, looking both amused and slightly intimidated. "Right." He gave a longing look back at the book, clearly eager to resume his lunch break reading. He quickly said, "I'm afraid the bank is closed for lunch. It'll open back up at two."

Sam said, "Really? Wow, I really messed that up. If it's okay, I'll just hang out with you until it opens again. I'll keep forgetting to deposit this check unless I do it now."

He was getting a resigned expression now. "There's an app that works amazingly well. For future reference, you know. It'll save you a trip."

"Oh, I prefer going to the bank. I figure it's a good way to provide the tellers with job security."

Gerald gave a small sigh and put his book down after carefully slipping in a bookmark. "True," he said. He frowned. "Listen, I'm sorry about the first book club meeting going sideways like that. I promise it's not always that way."

"I was sure it wasn't. Otherwise, there wouldn't be any members left."

Gerald gave a small smile at this. "I meant more about Margaret's behavior. She was kind of over-the-top at the meeting. But you're right—the club wouldn't be around for long if we kept losing members at that rate. Poor Margaret."

The last bit had been said almost as an afterthought. And Sam noticed again that word of Margaret's demise had spread like wildfire. "It was fine. I like being around different types of people, and I heard she always made interesting points during the book discussions. I'm sorry she's gone."

Gerald tilted his head to one side. "Someone told me you were there when Margaret was discovered. Was that true?" His eyes were a bit suspicious as if Sam had deliberately joined book club with the sole purpose of murdering Margaret Brennan during the meeting.

"It was. Charlotte and I are friends. She'd invited me to come to the shop when she opened to help revamp her social media presence for Twice-Told Tales. Unfortunately, we never got that far." Sam made a mental reminder to check back in on Charlotte. Not only had she taken Margaret's death hard, but she also needed to see if she wanted to try to work on her social media again.

Gerald said, "And you and Charlotte found Margaret there. How did Charlotte miss her? Didn't she check around the shop before she closed up?"

It was almost as if Gerald suspected Charlotte of having something to do with Margaret's death. "No, Margaret was in the back room, where the meeting had been. I guess when everyone got up to purchase their books and head out, no one noticed she was left behind. Charlotte mentioned that everyone does a good job cleaning up after themselves so she'd planned on cleaning up anything remaining the next morning."

Gerald frowned. "Okay. Still sort of weird that Margaret was in there overnight." He leaned forward, lowering his voice as if someone might somehow hear them in the deserted parking lot. "Has anyone mentioned Charlotte's financial situation?"

He definitely appeared to be trying to implicate Charlotte. Sam felt naturally defensive since Charlotte was a friend. Sadly, she wasn't surprised to hear Twice-Told Tales might be going through some tough times. After all, the store had weathered a hurricane, and the repairs hadn't been cheap. She remembered Charlotte had said there was no flood insurance on the shop, so she'd had to pay for a lot of the repairs herself. Still, she tried to keep an open mind and hear Gerald out. "Is Charlotte's store in trouble?"

"I don't know if it's in *trouble*, but it's struggling. The book club is a way for her to drive traffic and sales to the shop. Not only do we order the club's books at her shop, a lot of us will buy another book or two while we're over there."

Sam said, "What does this have to do with Margaret's death?"

"Margaret kept scaring people away. Charlotte tried to talk with her about it, but she refused to change. I heard Charlotte tell Claire that if Margaret kept it up, there wouldn't be a book club to run. Not everyone was as tolerant of Margaret's behavior as you were, especially as a new member." He pushed his glasses up. "Could you tell how she died?"

Sam quickly shook her head. "That's something forensics is looking into."

"It's just that Charlotte had the most opportunity, didn't she? She would have been at the store after we all left, to close up."

Sam said, "The police weren't convinced it was foul play. Of course, they had to treat Margaret's death as suspicious. But she might have died from natural causes."

"Oh, okay. Well, maybe that's a possibility, then. Margaret did have a heart condition."

Sam said, "She did?"

"Definitely. You should have seen her at last month's meeting. We read *The Cardiac Protocol*. It was this medical thriller. Not a bad book. But Margaret found all kinds of reasons to hate it. Although she'd said the medication part of the story was accurate. She over-shared about her heart medications and blood pressure prescriptions."

Sam nodded. Maybe it had been a natural death, after all. It sounded like she'd had a hard time regulating her blood pressure. She'd see if Aiden had more information from his police source later on. Surely by this point, the medical examiner should have been able to glean more information about Margaret's death. "Well, I'm sorry she's gone. And Charlotte seemed very upset, too."

"I'm sure she *seemed* that way. But her life will be a lot easier with Margaret out of the way."

Sam said, "If it was actually foul play, who do you think might have been responsible? Any ideas? I'm sure you must know everyone pretty well."

"I can't really picture anyone doing it. And you know I'm not saying Charlotte had anything to do with Margaret's death. She was always very congenial with her."

Sam said, "Did anyone in the club have an especially tough time with Margaret?"

Gerald considered this as he munched what looked like a peanut butter and jelly sandwich. "I guess I'd have to say Sofia always acts a little shifty."

"Shifty? I thought she was just shy. She seemed very friendly, though."

Gerald said, "Yeah, she's probably shy. But she was especially uncomfortable around Margaret. Like she wanted to talk to her but *didn't* want to at the same time."

"Maybe she thought Margaret had good feedback? Could she have just been interested in her insights on the selections?"

Gerald shrugged again. "Who knows? Maybe." He looked back again at his book.

Sam said, "Did you notice anybody lingering behind at the shop after the meeting was over?"

"Nope. That's because I didn't linger, myself. I don't have any idea who might have stayed behind. The police have already asked me about that." He made a face. "I guess they need to talk to everybody at book club."

Gerald gave a regretful glance at his watch. "Well, that's the end of my break. If you want to come back in, I'll open up my window again. We'll get that check of yours deposited. But you really should consider online banking. It's so much more conve-nient."

Sam totally agreed.

Chapter Seven

It was much later in the afternoon when Sam headed over to Aiden's house. As instructed, she brought Arlo with her. The evening air was cool as they walked the few blocks to Aiden's house. The craftsman bungalow glowed with warm light from within, and smoke curled from the chimney. Even from the sidewalk, Sam could smell something delicious cooking.

Aiden opened the door before she could knock, as if he'd been watching out for them. He wore jeans and a navy Henley that brought out his eyes, his dark hair slightly damp as if he'd just showered after school.

"Right on time," he said with a smile that made Sam's stomach flutter in a way she chose to ignore. "Come on in. It's getting cold out there."

Arlo trotted inside immediately, making himself at home. Aiden crouched down to greet him, producing a dog treat from his pocket. "Hey, buddy. I didn't forget about you."

Arlo took the treat from him politely, carefully putting his teeth on it so he wouldn't accidentally nip Aiden's hand. He settled in front of the fire with it.

Sam smiled at Aiden. "It smells amazing in here."

"I hope you like chili. I made cornbread, too."

Sam followed him through the living room, taking in all the details she'd been too polite to study on previous visits. Built-in bookshelves lined one wall, packed with an eclectic mix of crime novels, local history, teaching materials, and what looked like poetry collections. Black and white photographs of Sunset Ridge's historic buildings decorated the walls—his own work, she remembered.

The kitchen was warm and inviting, with original cabinetry painted a soft sage green and a farmhouse table by the window. He'd set two places with simple pottery bowls and cloth napkins.

"Can I help?" Sam asked.

"Absolutely not. You've been interrogating suspects all day. At least, that's what I'm guessing. Just sit." He poured her a glass of red wine without asking if she wanted it, then fixed himself the same. "How did it go today?"

Sam settled into a chair. "It was good. I ran into Nora when I was walking Arlo. Unsurprisingly, she had ideas about how I should do my investigating. One of them was actually helpful, though. She told me Gerald's usual lunch habits." Aiden looked confused, and Sam clarified. "Sorry. That's Gerald Parker. He's one of the book club members and works as a bank teller."

"Was it a good conversation?" Aiden ladled chili into bowls and brought over a basket of warm cornbread.

"It was a strange one. He seemed both reluctant to talk with me and very nervous. He spent half the conversation trying to implicate Charlotte."

"Really? That's interesting."

"Right?" asked Sam. "Because killing a book club member wouldn't exactly be a good way to drum up business for the store." She took a bite of the chili and closed her eyes. "Wow. This is amazing."

"Family recipe. My grandma would disown me if I didn't make it properly." Aiden sat across from her, his long legs stretching out under the table. "So Gerald's deflecting. What's your gut say?"

Sam said ruefully, "My gut is kind of going back and forth. I think he's hiding something, but I don't think it's murder." Sam wrapped her hands around the warm bowl. "I'm not sure what it is. He also mentioned Sofia, saying she'd been very nervous around Margaret lately."

"Sofia?"

Sam said, "She's apparently a fairly new member. A grad student at Western Carolina." Sam took another bite. "What would you do next, if you were still a detective?"

"I'd start out with background checks on everyone, starting with whoever's acting most suspicious." Aiden studied her across the table. "But you're not a detective, and I'm pretty sure Chief Hawkins wouldn't appreciate you running criminal checks."

"Probably not," agreed Sam. "He didn't seem especially happy to see me at Twice-Told Tales yesterday morning. I guess he thinks I have a nasty habit of discovering bodies. He'd like me to back off."

"But you won't."

"Probably not," agreed Sam cheerfully. "Do you miss it? Being a detective, I mean?"

Aiden considered this, cutting his cornbread into pieces. "Sometimes. I miss the puzzle-solving and the moment when everything clicks into place. But I don't miss the darkness. Or the things people do to each other." He met her eyes. "Teaching is better for my soul, I think."

"That makes sense."

"Besides," he added with a slight smile. "I can still help solve the occasional murder. Just from a safe distance."

After they'd finished eating, Sam spotted a book on the kitchen counter. She recognized the cover right away.

"You're reading *Middlemarch*? That's our book club selection this month."

Aiden said, "I saw it on Charlotte's website. I don't have time to do the book club meetings during the school year because I'm usually grading papers, but I thought maybe we could read the same books and talk about them." He looked almost shy. "I hope that's not weird."

"No, it isn't, it's . . . " Sam searched for the right word. Sweet? Thoughtful? Slightly overwhelming in the best way possible? "It's really nice, actually. What do you think of it so far?"

"I'm liking it more than I expected to." Aiden leaned back in his chair. "I mean, it's dense. I'm only on page sixty-something, but Eliot's prose is gorgeous. And the way she writes about provincial life, with all these people trapped by their circumstances and expectations feels almost modern."

"Yes!" Sam leaned forward, animated now. "And Dorothea is so idealistic, but you can already see how that idealism is going to trap her. The dramatic irony is painful."

Aiden smiled. "You're further along than I am, aren't you?"

"Early 200s," Sam admitted.

"Of course you are." But his tone was affectionate. "Are you going to keep reading at that pace, though?"

"I don't know. It's 880 pages. I just want to be prepared for the discussion."

"Sam, the book club meeting is weeks away."

"I know. But I'm enjoying it, too. That's keeping me reading. And I've been busily writing notes in the margins as I go when different thoughts pop into my head. It's the sign of a good book for me."

"You write in the margins?"

Sam flushed. She felt like it was another very Type-A thing she did. She couldn't even enjoy a book without marking it up with notes. "I know. It's kind of excessive."

"No, it's not. It's you engaging with the story." Aiden's voice was gentle. "I'd love to see your copy of the book after you're done. I bet your notes are fascinating."

"They're probably just neurotic," said Sam dismissively. But she was smiling. "I track character development, note any incon-sistencies, and sometimes have full arguments with the author in the margins."

"It seems more passionate than neurotic. Did you ever think about teaching? Maybe literature?"

"No, I'm too Type-A for that. I'd have wanted to control how the students interpreted the text." She laughed at herself. "Which is, I realize, completely the opposite of what good teaching should be."

They talked about books for another hour, their conver-sation ranging from favorites to guilty pleasures, to the books they'd been assigned in school and hated. Aiden told her about trying to get his students excited about things he'd enjoyed reading in high school, even though he was a technology teacher. "Maybe I should have been an English teacher, after all."

"I really enjoyed my high school English classes. Although I never finished *Moby Dick*."

"It's okay," Aiden said solemnly. "No one actually finished *Moby Dick*. We all just pretend."

"Thank you," said Sam with mock seriousness. "I've been carrying that shame for years."

The fire had burned down to embers, and Arlo was snoring softly on the rug. Sam realized she'd been there for nearly three hours, but it felt like minutes. She couldn't remember the last time she'd been this comfortable with someone.

"I probably should go," she said reluctantly. "It's getting late."

"Or," Aiden said, then paused. "Sorry. I was going to suggest we could watch a movie or something, but I might be keeping you from something you need to do."

Sam laughed. "Oh, I've got lists waiting for me at home. I always do."

They both stood, and suddenly the space between them felt smaller, more charged. Aiden carefully reached out and gently touched her arm.

"Sam," he started. Then Arlo chose that moment to wake up, giving a huge, noisy yawn and stretch, breaking the tension.

They both laughed, and the moment passed. But the warmth remained.

Aiden walked them to the door. "Thanks for coming over. For the company, I mean. Not just for talking about what happened at the bookstore."

"Thanks for the chili. And for reading the book with me." Sam clipped Arlo's leash on. "That was really thoughtful."

"Anytime." He meant it, she could tell.

As Sam and Arlo walked home, she found herself smiling.

Arlo looked up at her, his expression knowing. "Don't say it," Sam warned him. "We're just friends."

Maybe.

Chapter Eight

For whatever reason, Sam had a tough time sleeping that night. It was hard to imagine because it had been a huge day, starting with the discovery of poor Margaret, progressing through speaking with a couple of different suspects, then ending up at Aiden's. She'd given up on sleep around 2 a.m. and spent the rest of the night reading *Middlemarch* instead. The book was both an escape and homework. It was pages and pages of Victorian society, complex relationships, and buried secrets. She was on page 414 now, her purple pen busy in the margins. She'd marked passages about Dorothea's idealistic naivety with yellow tabs.

Arlo, giving an exasperated huff, jumped off the bed and headed off to a corner of the room for a more restful sleep. Later, when she'd gotten up, her morning exercise was sloppy at best, and she cut quite a few corners. Then, when she looked in her fridge, she found her breakfast options uninspiring. It hadn't been the best day so far. She felt like she needed to hit the reset button and turn it back around again.

"I think I'm going to run out to the coffeehouse," she announced to Arlo. He gave her a hopeful look. "Sorry, they don't allow dogs there, which is very short-sighted of them. I'll be back soon, love."

Sam remembered on the way over that she'd seen Sofia Smith from book club work at the coffee shop sometimes. Or maybe that was the underlying reason why she found herself on her way over there. She wondered if Sofia was working today or if it was one of the days she was in her grad classes. Of course, the problem was that it was morning, and she'd likely be busy even if she was working.

Mountain Perk Coffee Shop occupied a narrow storefront on Main Street with exposed brick walls, mismatched vintage furniture, and the rich aroma of freshly ground beans. Local art hung salon-style near a community bulletin board cluttered with flyers and business cards.

Sam found herself lucky on two counts; Sofia was working, and the shop wasn't busy at all. Sofia was behind the counter, wiping down the espresso machine. She looked exhausted, her eyes red-rimmed. She tensed slightly when she saw Sam, then gave her a tight smile. "Hi," Sofia said. "Sam, isn't it? From book club?"

Sam nodded. "That's right. You're Sofia?"

The young woman nodded. "What can I get for you today?"

Sam ordered an espresso, feeling like she needed the extra caffeine. Then, instead of taking a seat, she stood there to wait.

Sofia said quietly, "What did you think of book club?" Her hands were shaking slightly as she made the espresso.

"I thought everybody's opinions on the books really gave me a lot more insight into the story than I got on my own," said Sam truthfully.

Sofia nodded. "You're planning on coming back next month? I mean considering everything? I guess you heard what happened." Her voice caught slightly on the last words.

"I did. I was really sorry about Margaret."

An expression Sam couldn't really read passed across Sofia's features. "I was too. Although we might have been the only ones."

"Oh, I don't think that's true. It sounded to me like Margaret contributed a lot to the discussions. It's always good to have dissenting views."

"She definitely had those," said Sofia.

"You must really love reading. I'm sure you're probably swamped with stuff you have to read for your graduate studies."

Their conversation was interrupted as a customer came in. Sofia seemed almost relieved by the interruption. Sofia said to them, "The usual?" The customer nodded, and Sofia said, "I'll get it for you in just a minute."

Sam said, "I'm sorry to bother you. I guess I'm just trying to process everything."

Sofia slid her espresso in front of her, and Sam paid up. Sofia said, "I get it. How about if I take a seat with you after I get this order done? We can talk about it a little. It's been pretty slow this morning, anyway."

"I'll sit at the bar then. That'll be easier for you."

Sam watched as Sofia swiftly and competently got the customer's drink prepared, although her movements seemed almost mechanical, as if she was just going through the motions. After checking his order out, she stood back in front of Sam at the bar. "You were asking why I joined book club."

Sam gave her a smile. "Sorry, I must sound really nosy. I was just thinking you were already snowed under with books you had to read for school."

"True. But I wanted to meet people. I'm new to the area."

Sofia looked away. It felt to Sam like she was concealing something, although she wasn't sure why she'd react that way to such an innocuous question.

"Why did *you* join?" asked Sofia, turning the tables.

"Actually, for the same reasons. I'm still new to Sunset Ridge, and I wanted to get more involved and meet people. Also, I wanted to show Charlotte some support."

Sofia's expression softened at this. "Yeah, Charlotte's great. She's been really nice to me."

Sam nodded. "I've been in a kind of reading rut too. Just reading the same things. I thought joining the book club would be a good way for me to enjoy something totally different. Maybe I can find a new genre to read."

Sofia gave her a rueful look. "You picked the wrong time to join, didn't you? I guess the police have spoken with you, too?" She pushed a cleaning rag over the surface of the already-clean bar. She'd made the question sound casual, but Sam noticed the tightening of her muscles, as if she really wanted to know.

"Yes, I've spoken with them. Actually, Charlotte and I were the ones who discovered poor Margaret. So the police were talking with us right away."

Sofia stiffened. "You were there when she was found?"

"That's right. Charlotte had asked me to come by when she opened so we could work on her social media branding. It was quite a shock. Charlotte especially took it hard, because she'd known Margaret for a while."

Sofia nodded at this. "Was she at the shop the whole night?"

"I'm afraid she was. At least, it sure looks that way."

Sofia immediately said, "I went straight home after the meeting. I had a project I needed to work on."

"I get the impression that maybe she died before anyone actually left the building. But that's just a guess." Sam paused. "What did you make of Margaret?" asked Sam carefully.

"She was intense. Really critical. I don't like speaking ill of the dead, but she was a hard person to like. I don't think anyone in the group did." Her voice softened a little. "Except Charlotte, maybe. But Charlotte is always really generous with everyone."

Sam quietly sipped her espresso for a moment, thinking the pause might make Sofia continue. Which, eventually, it did.

"I wanted us to focus on some lighter reading," said Sofia finally. "You know, something fun and engaging. But Margaret didn't want that. She made me feel stupid for even suggesting it. Having Margaret around made everyone uncomfortable. It made us all second-guess our opinions about a book or offering up anything to begin with, since she was going to shoot them down. She was just really critical and harsh. It made us all pretty tense."

"I'm sorry. It sounds like a really tough atmosphere for an honest exchange of ideas. It's terrible what happened to Margaret, but it sounds like the book club meetings, in some ways, might grow for the better."

Sofia bobbed her head. "That's totally true." She absent-mindedly wiped down an area of the bar that she'd already cleaned. "Margaret had a bad effect on everybody. Dylan, especially."

"He's the poet, isn't he?"

Sofia took a deep breath. "He wants to be."

"Did he share any of his work with Margaret?" Sam winced inwardly at this. She hoped he hadn't, in some ways. Margaret certainly wasn't the most nurturing of reviewers. And the young man had seemed vulnerable to her in some ways.

"He knew better than to do that. He'd seen what happened when Claire talked about writing romance. But he had an open mic night. Right over there," said Sofia, gesturing to a corner of the store where the shop would host performers. "I wasn't working that night, but I heard about it. It was a real disaster."

Another couple of customers came in, and Sofia spent the next ten minutes taking care of their orders. Sam thought about how discouraging Margaret had been to the nascent talent of the younger book club members. It wasn't ever easy to have your dreams dashed like that. Was it enough to murder someone over, though? Maybe in the heat of the moment, but if Margaret had been poisoned?

After Sofia wrapped up the orders, she stood in front of Sam again.

"You were talking about Dylan," Sam said.

Sofia made a dismissive gesture. "I don't really know anything about it. Like I said, I wasn't here. But I know he was really crushed by Margaret's reaction to his poetry. He mentioned quitting the club. I was glad he stuck around."

Sam circled back to something that had been bothering her. "You said Margaret made you feel stupid for suggesting lighter reading? It sounds like she did that often? Made people feel small?"

Sofia's hands stilled on the milk pitcher she'd been wiping. For just a moment, her carefully neutral expression cracked.

"She did it her whole life." The words came out sharp, almost bitter. Then, Sofia seemed to catch herself, softening her tone. "I mean, from what I heard. From the other members. That Margaret was always that way."

"You've heard stories about her from before the book club?" asked Sam.

"Just . . . you know. It's a small town. People talk. Charlotte mentioned Margaret had been teaching for like thirty years. That's a lot of students who probably have stories."

"Did you know her from before?" asked Sam. "From the university, maybe? Before she retired?"

"No." The answer was quick, defensive. Sofia busied herself with rearranging the cup lids that didn't need rearranging. "I didn't know her. But I've known people like her. Professors who think tearing other people down is the same as teaching."

Then the door opened as another customer walked in, and Sofia's professional mask slid back into place. Sam turned to see that the customer was Chief Hawkins. He spotted Sam immediately. "Ms. Prescott. You're everywhere, aren't you?"

"Just getting coffee."

"Uh-huh. Just try to leave some investigating for the actual police." In his voice was a weary acceptance.

Before she could answer, Hawkins was chatting with Sofia. Sam decided this might be the perfect opportunity to ask him a few questions. But not in front of Sofia. She quietly finished her coffee, waved to the barista, then left to sit at a table outside the coffeehouse to wait for her quarry.

Hawkins followed a few minutes later with his coffee in hand.

"So," he said, taking a sip. "Sofia Smith. What did you learn?"

"Like I said, I was just visiting with her. She's a member of my book club, after all. I'm trying to get to know everyone."

"Right." Hawkins waited.

Sam sighed. "I didn't learn much. She said she barely knew Margaret because Sofia's a new member. She left when everyone else did and went back home to work on a grad school project."

"Which matches what she told us," said Hawkins.

Sam hesitated. There was something off with Sofia, but she couldn't put her finger on it. "She seemed really stressed out. That could just be school, work, and the fact she's now caught up in an investigation." She paused. "Which I'm assuming is a murder inquiry."

Hawkins frowned at her. "What makes you assume that?"

"The fact you're pressing me on what I heard from Sofia."

Hawkins sighed. "Margaret's death was suspicious. You were right about that."

"Was it poisoned? The coffee, I mean?"

He nodded. "That's right. Although I'm still curious how you came to that conclusion. You're sure you didn't know Margaret Brennan?"

"Not at all. I hadn't met her before book club. Our paths hadn't crossed whatsoever."

"Kind of odd in a small town," said Hawkins. He took another sip of coffee. "Look, I know I can't stop you from asking questions around town. But when you learn something relevant, I need to know. This isn't a game. And you could get hurt."

"I know that."

"Do you?" His voice was gentle but firm. "Because somebody killed Margaret Brennan, and killers don't appreciate amateur detectives getting too close to the truth."

"I'm careful."

"That's what worries me. You're pretty good at this, and you don't know when to quit." He sighed. "Just watch your back. And call me if you find anything solid."

"I will."

Hawkins headed toward his cruiser, and Sam turned toward her car. As she did, she glanced back at Mountain Perk.

Through the plate-glass window, Sofia stood at the counter, clearly visible. Watching Sam with a thoughtful expression on her face.

Chapter Nine

Sam ran a few errands after that, but her mind kept running through what she'd learned that morning. Then she thought about Charlotte again, and how upset she'd been at finding Margaret. Maybe she'd bring her some food.

After running by the grocery store, Sam made a quick trip to her house to put all her purchases away. Then she stopped by Mountain View Deli to pick up two turkey clubs with all the fixings and a couple of bags of chips. She knew Charlotte liked their sweet tea, so she grabbed two of those as well.

The "closed" sign still hung in Twice-Told Tales' front window when Sam arrived. She knocked gently, and Charlotte appeared a moment later, unlocking the door.

"You're a lifesaver," Charlotte said, her voice weary. She looked tired, with dark circles under her eyes and her hair pulled back in a messy ponytail. "Come on in."

They settled into a couple of chairs in the main room of the store. Charlotte sighed. "I couldn't bring myself to open the store yet. It somehow feels sort of disrespectful to Margaret. But I will tomorrow. I know I can't stay closed forever."

"Finding Margaret like that was so rough, I know." Sam split up the food and drinks between them. "How are you really doing?"

Charlotte unwrapped her sandwich eagerly, as if she'd forgotten to eat. "I keep replaying it. I should have checked the back room before I locked up. Maybe if I'd found her sooner, she wouldn't have died."

"You couldn't have known she was still there. Nobody could."

"No, you're right," said Charlotte. "Logically, I know that." Charlotte took a bite, chewing mechanically. "But I keep thinking about her being alone all night. Even if she was already gone." Charlotte swallowed. "It just feels wrong."

Sam said, "I know."

They quietly ate their lunch for a few moments. Then Charlotte said, "Officer Martinez was very kind. Very professional, but not cold, you know? She took my statement and asked if I needed anything." She took a sip of her sweet tea. "The chief spent more time peppering me with questions about who had access to the building, whether anyone seemed upset, and where everyone was during the meeting. He also wanted to know who left when."

"What did you tell him?"

Charlotte sighed. "You saw how it was. There were people at the cash register, buying books. People chatting. Members were coming and going. But I did notice Dylan left almost the second we finished. And that's not like him at all. Usually he lingers, wants to talk about the books, and ask for reading recommendations. But after the meeting, he couldn't get out fast enough."

"Do you think he was just uncomfortable? Margaret was being really critical of everyone."

Charlotte shook her head slowly. "It was more than that. He looked almost scared. Or angry, maybe. I couldn't tell which." She paused. "What I didn't mention to the police, because I didn't think of it later, was that Dylan had been one of Margaret's students. It was years ago at Western Carolina."

"Wow. He probably knew exactly how she was going to act at book club."

"Right," said Charlotte. "He mentioned it once when he first joined the club. Dylan said something about having her as a professor and hoping she wouldn't remember him. Then, with what happened on open mic night?" Charlotte made a face. "I feel awful about that. Almost like I should have been able to protect him better."

"What happened?"

Charlotte said, "Dylan was so excited. He'd been working on honing his poetry for weeks. He was really shy when he invited us all to go to the coffeehouse one night for their open mic night." She sighed again. "I mean, the whole point of those types of events is to build community for local artists and help build them up. But Margaret eviscerated him."

"Oh no."

Charlotte gave a sad nod. "In front of everyone. She said his work showed 'the dangers of participation-trophy-culture meeting poetry.' The local press was there covering it; you know how they always write-up small town events. Anyway, they quoted her. Dylan was devastated."

"That's incredibly brutal."

Charlotte said, "And his girlfriend broke up with him over it."

Sam frowned. "Really? That's ridiculous."

"Well, that's what Dylan said to me. Apparently, she was embarrassed to be seen with him after the article in the paper came out."

"That's a pretty strong motive," said Sam slowly.

"I know." Charlotte looked miserable. "That's why I told Chief Hawkins about it. But Sam, I've known Dylan over a year. He's passionate about his creativity, and he can be intense. But I can't see him murdering anybody."

"Maybe it was just the straw breaking the camel's back?"

"I suppose." Charlotte took another bite of her sandwich, chewing thoughtfully for a few moments. "Then Gerald called me this morning."

"What did he want?"

Charlotte said, "He was worried because he thought you might suspect him. He mentioned that the two of you had spoken during his lunch break at the bank. He wanted to make sure you knew he didn't do anything wrong." She sighed. "Gerald's got his secrets. I mean, everyone does. But he's not violent. He's just anxious, I think. Whatever he's hiding, it's not murder."

"Do you have any idea what Gerald is hiding?"

Charlotte shook her head. "It's nothing that would lead to murder, Sam. I'm certain of that."

Was Charlotte's judgment clouded by her friendship with him?

"There was one other thing that struck me as odd yesterday. About Pamela."

"The retired librarian?" asked Sam.

"Right. I saw her at the library yesterday afternoon. I like to go in there sometimes to read some of the national papers. Pamela is often in the library, even though she no longer works there. Anyway, Pamela was in the reading room, just sitting there staring at nothing. When she got up to leave, I could tell she'd been crying. Her eyes were all red and puffy, mascara smudged." She shook her head. "Pamela's usually so composed and put-together. I've never seen her like that."

Sam asked, "Did you talk to her?"

"I wanted to, but she left before I could catch her. She was definitely not herself."

Sam made a mental note to talk to Pamela. "Do you know if she and Margaret had any history? Beyond book club, I mean?"

"I don't think so. But Pamela's pretty private. She doesn't share much about her personal life." Charlotte picked at the corner of her sandwich wrapper. "Actually, now that I think about it, Pamela usually helps me clean up after meetings. She's always been really considerate that way. But after book club, she didn't even say goodbye. She just left."

Charlotte frowned, then added, "Gerald kind of scampered away, too. I felt sure he was going to follow up on collecting dues at the end of the meeting."

It seemed to Sam that everyone had been off that night. And Margaret was now dead.

"Sam." Charlotte's voice pulled her back to the present. "I need to say something, and I don't want you to take it the wrong way."

"Okay." Sam looked curiously at her friend.

"It's just that I think you should back off and let the police handle this. Really. I know you like to figure things out, and you're good at it. But somebody killed Margaret. Gerald has already noticed you're poking around in this, and it won't be long before others do, too. I don't want you getting hurt."

Sam studied Charlotte. Was Charlotte trying to protect her? Or was she trying to protect someone else? "I'm just talking to people. I'm sure the other book club members are probably doing the same thing. I promise I'll be careful."

Through the bookstore's front window, Sam glimpsed Dylan Morrison walking past on the sidewalk. He had his hands shoved deep in his jacket pockets, his head down against the wind.

Charlotte noticed Sam's gaze and followed it. "Dylan," she called out, tapping on the window and gesturing for him to come in.

He hesitated, clearly spotting Sam through the glass. For a moment, Sam though he might pretend he hadn't heard and keep walking. But Charlotte was already heading to the door, opening it.

"Come in for a minute," Charlotte said. "I've been meaning to call you."

Dylan's eyes met Sam's through the doorway, and something flickered across his face. Was it wariness or resignation? He came inside.

Chapter Ten

Charlotte gave him a cheerful greeting, but Dylan still seemed uneasy. Charlotte quickly said, "Hey, I got that new poetry collection. The Kaveh Akbar one. You'd been asking about it."

Dylan's features cleared. "Oh, thanks. I've been wanting to read it."

"I kept it behind the register for you. Just in case there are other big poetry fans out here in Sunset Ridge." She gave him a wink as if to say she seriously doubted it.

Charlotte handed him the book, and Dylan almost reverently started turning the pages. Then he hastily pulled out some crumpled bills from his wallet, handing them to Charlotte. "Thanks. I can't wait to read it."

She gave him his change, and Dylan looked as if he might hurry off. Then he seemed to focus back on Charlotte. "I heard what happened. Are you okay? That must have been . . . " He seemed to search for a word before settling on one. "Upsetting."

Charlotte nodded. "It was. And still very unsettling." She gestured to Sam. "Sam was with me, too."

Dylan gave Sam a sympathetic look. "I'm sorry. Sorry for you both. What an awful thing to have happened. I mean, Margaret was challenging, but I never wished her any harm. Was it a heart attack?"

That seemed to be the ailment of choice everyone had chosen to explain Margaret's death. But then, Margaret had told everyone she was on heart medication.

Charlotte looked over at Sam. Sam said, "The police are treating it as a suspicious death."

"*Are* they?" Dylan paled. "You're saying she was murdered?"

Sam nodded.

Dylan said, "What, like someone broke into the shop and killed Margaret?"

Charlotte shook her head. "It sounds like Margaret might have been murdered at the end of book club. That's right, isn't it, Sam?"

"That's what it sounds like."

Dylan sat down heavily in a chair. "I had no idea. I thought she had suffered some kind of natural death. That was bad enough." He swallowed. "So the police are involved?"

Sam said, "Yes. I'm sure they'll probably be speaking with everyone who was at book club. Have they reached out to you, yet?"

"No." He sighed. "This is awful. I bet the cops are going to focus on me right away. The whole town knows Margaret savaged me in the newspaper after the open mic night."

Charlotte firmly said, "That's not true. Not everyone reads the paper. And even the subscribers don't read every story."

"Sure, but it won't take much for the cops to search Margaret's name and have the article come up." He paused. "Did the police say how they thought she died?" He frowned. "Or could you tell? Were there, like, marks on her neck or a head wound or something?"

Charlotte shook her head. "I didn't see anything like that. Did you, Sam?"

"Nothing."

Dylan said slowly, "So, do they think she was poisoned, then? If she wasn't strangled and didn't have any head trauma?"

"I guess that's something forensics is going to have to determine," said Sam.

Dylan said, "I wasn't anywhere around her tea."

"It was actually coffee," said Charlotte.

"Whatever. Whatever she was drinking, I wasn't near it. Like I said, Margaret was pretty challenging. I do my best to just stay away from her whenever I can. So I wasn't beside her."

Although Sam did remember Margaret talking briefly to Dylan before the meeting started. He'd looked tense. Had Margaret been holding her coffee then? Had it been unattended? She couldn't remember.

Dylan continued, "I left right after the meeting was done, too. I couldn't get out of there fast enough." He gave Charlotte an apologetic look. "Sorry. I love book club. I just wasn't crazy about Margaret. I went home, and was working on revising my poems until something like two a.m."

Sam said, "That's real dedication."

He shrugged. "I want to prove to myself that I wasn't what she said I was. That I'm better than just a hack poet. But nobody can confirm that, though, so I won't have an alibi for the cops. I live by myself in a studio apartment." He sighed. "I have a hard time thinking of anybody in book club being a killer."

"What did everyone else make of Margaret?" asked Sam.

Dylan gave a short laugh. "They all liked her about as much as I did. I know Claire can't stand her, although she's tried hard to, considering she's the club president. Gerald always looked kind of sick whenever Margaret was around. He looked especially ill when Margaret talked about writing her memoir last month."

Sam raised her eyebrows. "Margaret was a writer?"

"Well, she fancied herself one. Considering what a perfectionist Margaret was, I'm not sure how far along she got with her book. Pamela wasn't fond of hearing about the memoir, either. Maybe she thought Margaret was going to behave even worse at book club if she became a published author. It's hard to *imagine* Margaret being worse, but I guess it's possible. I wouldn't have liked it, either. I'd love to get a chapbook published."

Sam said, "Are you able to work on your writing full-time?" She had the feeling this wasn't the case, but wondered if Dylan's parents might be playing the role of patrons.

Dylan gave another abrupt laugh. "I wish. I've been working at the community center. I teach a beginners creative writing course and a poetry workshop. Aside from that, I get a few hours waiting tables at a restaurant downtown."

"The workshops sound like fun. Do you enjoy teaching?" asked Sam.

Dylan looked pleased. "I like using my MFA. That's a Master of Fine Arts."

"Wow, good for you," said Sam. "I've heard those are tough to get."

Charlotte gave Dylan a proud look. "He's even gotten a grant from the local arts council for teaching underserved populations."

"A small grant," said Dylan modestly. "But it's nice to get the support while doing something I love."

"Do you have any workshops coming up?" asked Sam. "I've always thought a writing class would be fun to take. Not that I'd ever be serious with writing, but I like trying new things."

"Not right now. I just finished a session. Spring workshops are on hold due to budget cuts. But I can let you know if that changes."

"Thanks."

Dylan glanced at his watch. "I'd better head out now. Good talking to you both. Take it easy; you deserve it after finding Margaret."

After Dylan walked out, Charlotte shook her head. "I worry about Dylan, I have to admit. He's such a sensitive guy. I feel like the world just crushes him." She paused. "I wonder if the workshop was really canceled because of budget cuts."

"What do you think happened?"

Charlotte pursed her lips. "Maybe Dylan pulled out of it out of embarrassment. Maybe he thought no one would sign up for a creative writing or poetry course from someone who had such a public embarrassment like he did at the open mic night."

There was a loud beeping sound behind the shop, and Charlotte raised her hands in dismay. "I forgot about the book shipment."

"I need to get going, anyway. See you later, Charlotte."

Sam headed back home to take care of Arlo. It wasn't just Arlo, of course. Sam wanted to get all her thoughts out of her head and onto paper.

She pulled into her driveway, turned off the engine, and sat for a moment in the quiet. Through the front window, she could see Arlo's face pressed against the glass, his tail wagging so hard his whole body wiggled.

Inside, she was greeted with enthusiastic snuffles and circling. "I know, I know. I've been gone too long, haven't I?" Sam gave him a thorough ear rub before heading to the kitchen to refill his water bowl.

Her notebook sat on the kitchen table where she'd left it. She opened it and wrote "Book Club—What I Know."

She started with the obvious suspects: everyone who'd been at the meeting.

Claire Mills: Club President

- Motive: Margaret savagely critiqued her romance manuscript (years of work).
- Seems more hurt than angry. Too obvious?
- Pointed me toward Gerald.

Gerald Parker: Club Treasurer

- Motive??

- Behavior: Extremely nervous, evasive, deflecting
- Left book club quickly (unusual for him per Charlotte)
- Hiding something?
- Pointed me to Sofia

Dylan Morrison: Poet

- Motive: Public humiliation at open mic night
- Margaret gave a negative quote for an article in the local paper
- Works at the community center teaching creative writing and poetry
- Mentioned Gerald and Pamela disliking Margaret

Sofia Smith: Graduate Student

- Motive: ??? None apparent
- Behavior: Very evasive. Might know more about Margaret than she admits?
- New member to the club
- Claimed she went straight home to work on school project
- Pointed me toward Dylan

Pamela Cross: Retired Librarian

- Motive: ???
- Behavior: Haven't yet spoken with her. Only saw her at book club

- Dylan noticed she was uncomfortable hearing about Margaret's memoir, as did Gerald.
- Charlotte saw her at the library, crying. Left quickly after book club without saying goodbye.

It seemed like there might be more to learn about Margaret's memoir. Aiden's police friends might know something about its content if they'd searched Margaret's home. Chief Hawkins was unlikely to share anything with her, and she knew the state police wouldn't, if they were on the case by now.

The doorbell rang, making Sam jump. Arlo barked once, then trotted toward the front door, tail wagging. Not a threat, then.

Sam opened the door to find Nora, her sharp-tongued neighbor from down the street, standing on her porch, juggling a covered casserole dish in one hand while Precious strained at the leash in her other hand. The pit bull was wearing what appeared to be a small argyle sweater vest.

"Don't get excited, it's not for you," Nora said briskly to Arlo, who was wagging his tail. She tried to maneuver past Sam while Precious lunged forward to greet Arlo. The leash wrapped around Nora's legs. "Precious, for heaven's sake. Sam, a little help?"

Sam grabbed the casserole dish before Nora could drop it, pushed the door wider, and offered her arm to her. Arlo and Precious began their usual greeting ritual of sniffing and tail-wagging.

"Well, hello there, Arlo. At least someone's happy to see me," Nora said, unwinding herself from Precious's leash.

"I'm happy to see you," Sam said, closing the door. "I'm just surprised. Did we have plans?"

"No, but I saw your car pull up and figured you'd been out doing your amateur detective thing." Nora unclipped Precious's leash, and the pit bull immediately began his inspection of the living room while Arlo followed behind like a devoted admirer. Nora set her purse down and spotted Sam's notebook on the kitchen table. "Ah-ha! Making lists of suspects, are we?"

"Nora—"

"Don't Nora me. This is precisely what you do. Very organized, very thorough." She peered at the notebook before Sam could close it. "Ooh, you've got everyone listed, haven't you? Even Pamela. Who seems innocuous enough. And rather old."

Sam said, "I'm just trying to make sense of what happened."

"Mm-hmm." Nora opened Sam's refrigerator without asking and pulled out a bottle of sparkling water. "This casserole is for Edith Martin. She's at Sunset Ridge Senior Living, recovering from a hip replacement. I made her chicken and rice, which is basically invalid food, but that's what she requested."

"That's nice of you."

"I have my moments." Nora took a sip of water. "Anyway, I was going to drop it off, but then I thought you've probably been running around town all day talking to people. Have you eaten anything substantial?"

Sam wasn't sure that the granola bars she had for breakfast counted as substantial in Nora's eyes.

Nora gave a sniff as if she'd thought as much. "You could come with me to see Edith. Then we shall get an early dinner at that Italian place afterward."

"I hate to intrude on your visit with your friend."

"Please. Edith will love you. And Precious, of course. She's bored out of her mind, and all I'm going to do is drop off the casserole. She's not supposed to have long visits yet." Nora glanced at Sam's notebook again. "As I recall in my quick perusal of your notes, you were looking for a way to speak with Pamela."

Sam sighed. There seemed to be no point in denying it. "I'm just trying to get impressions from everyone who was at book club."

"Well then." Nora's eyes gleamed with interest. "Lucky for you, Pamela volunteers at Sunset Ridge Senior Living each week. She's in their library, for the most part, organizing book donations from the community. There's an excellent chance she'll be there right now. Completely coincidentally, of course."

Sam gave Nora a suspicious look. "You planned this, didn't you?"

"I simply planned to bring Edith her casserole. Of course, I *did* know Pamela volunteered there and that she was a book club member. The woman does love books. Anyway, what you do while you're at the retirement home is completely up to you." Nora called to Precious, who was now trying to climb onto Sam's couch despite his stocky build. "Come on, you ridiculous animal. We're leaving now, whether Sam comes or not."

"Let me grab my purse," said Sam. "Should I bring Arlo? For company?"

"Absolutely. The residents love seeing dogs." Nora was already clipping Precious's leash back on. "Besides, being accompanied by two dogs makes it look even less like you're there to interrogate anyone."

Chapter Eleven

Ten minutes later, Sam climbed into the back of Nora's sedan with Arlo, while Precious took his usual spot in the front passenger seat, gazing out the window with what could only be described as regal bearing. The casserole dish sat secured in a carrier between Sam's feet.

"I still think people should get precedence over dogs for the passenger seat," Sam said mildly as she buckled her seatbelt.

"Precious has seniority. He also suffers from motion sickness in the back," Nora replied, pulling out of Sam's driveway. "Besides, he likes to supervise."

Sam caught Precious's eye in the side mirror. The pit bull looked entirely too smug about the arrangement.

The facility was a sprawling single-story building designed to look less institutional and more like a collection of connected cottages. Someone had planted cheerful mums along the walkway, though they looked a bit bedraggled from the recent rain.

Nora climbed from her vehicle with the casserole dish while Precious immediately began investigating a particularly interesting patch of grass. Sam clipped Arlo's leash and joined them.

"Edith's in the west wing, Room 229," Nora announced. "The library is in the community room in the center building. That's where Pamela will be, assuming she's here today."

They made their way through the automatic doors into a lobby that smelled faintly of coffee and lemon-scented cleaning products. A young woman at the reception desk looked up with a welcoming smile.

"Hi, Nora! And you brought friends?" She came around the desk to greet Precious and Arlo. "Oh, aren't you both handsome boys? The residents are going to love seeing you."

"Hi Kendra," Nora said crisply. "I'm just dropping off dinner for Edith Marton. This is my neighbor, Sam Prescott."

"Nice to meet you," Sam said.

"Feel free to take the dogs around after you visit Edith," Kendra said. "Just check with the nurses first to make sure the residents are up for visitors."

They headed down the hallway, passing several residents in the common areas. A few called out greetings to Precious, who clearly was a regular visitor. In Room 229, they found Edith Martin sitting in a recliner with her leg elevated, watching a cooking show.

"Nora! You didn't have to do this," Edith said, though her face lit up. She was a tiny woman with snow-white hair and bright blue eyes behind wire-rimmed glasses.

"I thought you might want a little break from cafeteria food." Nora set the casserole in a small refrigerator. "This is Sam Prescott, my neighbor. And you remember Precious."

Precious, recognizing a friend, trotted over for ear scratches. Arlo, less confident, stayed close to Sam but wagged his tail hopefully.

"What a sweet little dog," Edith crooned. "Come here, honey."

Arlo needed no further invitation.

They chatted for a few minutes about Edith's recovery and the facility's food (which Edith insisted wasn't terrible). Then Sam, trying to sound casual, said, "Nora mentioned one of my book club members volunteers here. Pamela Cross?"

"Oh, Pamela! Yes, she's wonderful," Edith said, brightening. "She helps in the library every week. She used to be a teacher, you know. She's so patient with everyone."

"A librarian," Nora corrected gently. "Pamela was a librarian, not a teacher."

Edith blinked, then her cheeks flushed pink. "Oh dear, was she? I could have sworn . . . well, goodness." She chuckled at herself. "I'm always getting her mixed up with that other volunteer. The one who does the art classes on Thursdays. She was a teacher. An art teacher, I think."

"That's Evelyn Holmes," Nora supplied. "She teaches watercolors."

"Yes! That's who I was thinking of." Edith shook her head, still smiling. "My memory isn't what it used to be. But Pamela is lovely, whatever she used to do. She's been coming here for years. She always brings in new novels for our library and helps organize everything. She really knows her way around books."

Nora glanced at her watch with theatrical precision. "Well, we shouldn't tire you out. Doctor's orders were short visits only, correct?"

Edith rolled her eyes good-naturedly. "Yes, Nurse Nora. Thanks for the casserole and for the company."

Back in the hallway, Nora turned to Sam. "The library is just down this corridor and to the left. I believe I'll take Precious to see Mr. Holloway in the east wing. He does so enjoy Precious's company. You're welcome to come along. Or you might want to do something else?"

"I might just take Arlo to see if anyone in the library would like a visit."

"Excellent idea. I'll meet you back in the lobby in twenty minutes," said Nora.

Sam followed the signs to the community room, which housed a good-sized library along several walls. Comfortable chairs were scattered around, and afternoon sunlight streamed through large windows. A few residents sat reading, and at the far end, a woman was organizing books on a rolling cart. It was Pamela Cross.

She wore slacks and a cardigan, her gray hair pulled back into a neat bun. Reading glasses hung from a chain around her neck. She was methodically sorting books, checking the spines and arranging them with the careful attention of someone who genuinely loved what she was doing.

Sam hadn't planned exactly what she'd say. Taking a breath, she walked into the room with Arlo, who immediately drew attention from the two residents in the reading room.

Pamela glanced up. Her eyes met Sam's, and for just a moment, something flickered across her face. Surprise? Wariness? Then, her expression smoothed into polite pleasantness.

"Sam, isn't it?" she asked. "I'm surprised to see you here."

Sam smiled at her. "I'm here with my neighbor, Nora. But I stepped away to take a little tour of the facility."

Pamela said, "Oh, a reconnaissance mission? Are you thinking about having a parent move in?"

Sam quickly shook her head and then changed the subject. "No. But the library here is amazing. How long have you been volunteering?"

Pamela visibly relaxed as she talked for a few minutes about how the retirement home acquired books, how she managed the donations and organized the shelves, and other aspects of volunteering.

She paused as an elderly man walked up, greeting Pamela by name and asking for a book recommendation.

"Hi, Adam. Actually, there was a book that just came in that made me think of you."

Sam watched as Pamela and Adam chatted about John Grisham books as Pamela found a novel for him to check out.

Once the old man had left the library, Pamela walked back over to Sam. "It looks like a busy place," said Sam with a smile.

"It is. And often residents just like sitting in here, surrounded by books. It's one of my favorite rooms."

Sam said, "I'm not surprised. After all, I met you at a book club, and I know you were formerly a librarian for the county."

"That's right." Pamela's face darkened. "It looks like you joined book club at something of a tough time. Poor Margaret."

Pamela's body suddenly seemed much tenser. Sam said, "I'm sorry. I know you must have known her pretty well."

"What makes you say that?"

Sam said, "Just considering that you were in the same book club together. And I understand neither of you were new members."

"I see. Well, you're both correct and wrong. Correct in that she and I were long-standing members. However no one could say they knew Margaret well. Least of all me."

Sam asked, "She was a complex person?"

"Complex, yes. And a difficult individual." Pamela sighed. "Margaret was very critical of others, I'm afraid. I really shouldn't speak ill of her, considering what's happened, but it's the truth. Her absence will likely make club meetings easier for everyone."

"I see. I've known a few people like that. It sounded like she might have been hard on budding writers, too, from what I've heard. Maybe that's natural, considering her background as a professor."

Pamela pressed her lips together. "Is it natural? I think an English professor should be encouraging of his or her students instead of castigating them for the quality of their writing. Margaret seemed to think she herself was an excellent writer. I didn't see anything that made me believe that was the case."

"Oh, was Margaret working on something?"

Pamela's expression flickered. "She mentioned a memoir project. I don't know how far along she was with it." She paused, then added with what seemed like forced casualness, "Though knowing Margaret, she probably had strong opinions in it about everyone she'd ever met."

"That sounds about right," Sam said. "Did she talk about it at book club?"

"She just mentioned it once or twice, but she never went into the details. I try not to think about what Margaret might have been writing about the book club. I'm sure she wasn't complimentary." Pamela shrugged. "But the rest of the club talked about her memoir when Margaret wasn't around. We thought she'd be even more insufferable if she became a published author. Can you imagine? She was already impossible to deal with." She sighed. "I left book club meetings so completely stressed out. It's the opposite of the way discussing books should be."

"Relaxing and stimulating."

"Right," said Pamela. "Not stressful. You know, I'm not a young woman. I have a lot of heart-related issues that I'm treating with blood pressure medication and blood thinners. The stress from those meetings could have driven me into an early grave. I'm not exaggerating."

Sam nodded sympathetically. "I'd imagine that would be the case." She paused, choosing her words carefully. "Charlotte mentioned seeing you at the public library recently. She said she wanted to say hi, but you seemed preoccupied and hurried out. She was worried about you."

"The library?" She didn't meet Sam's eyes. "Oh, that. Yes. I wasn't feeling well that day. Just a terrible headache. I probably didn't even notice Charlotte was there." She gave a tight smile. "I'm better now, though."

Sam watched her for a moment. "That's good. Charlotte was concerned."

"Well, tell her I appreciate that, but there's no need to worry." Pamela's voice was firm now. She finally met Sam's gaze. "Have the police spoken with you? They questioned me about everything." Pamela tilted her head to one side. "Oh wait. You were with Charlotte when Margaret was found, weren't you? You poor thing. I really winced when I heard that. A brand-new member of our book club, too."

"Yes, I'm afraid I was there. But I was glad that Charlotte wasn't alone."

Pamela nodded gravely. "Yes, that would have been so much worse. What an absolutely horrible thing for Charlotte, though. First the hurricane caused so much damage to Twice-Told Tales. Then a suspicious death in her shop. At least, from what the authorities were saying, her death was suspicious." She paused. "Unfortunately, I wasn't able to help the police out much."

"I couldn't, either. I didn't notice anyone especially close to Margaret at the book club meeting."

Pamela said, "Exactly. Because who *wanted* to be close to her?" She sighed. "That's ungenerous of me. But Margaret could be a very difficult woman. If you engaged in conversation with her, she'd often turn a polite conversation into an argument." She leaned closer to Sam. "Could you tell how she died?" she asked quietly. "The police didn't disclose a cause of death. Did someone stay behind with her and murder her? Surely it wasn't Charlotte?"

"No. Even if Charlotte wanted to kill someone, she'd have the good sense not to do it in her own shop. It's looking like Margaret might have died before we all left the bookstore."

"Oh no. That's awful." Pamela winced. "I hate to think that. I hope her demise was fast. That she didn't suffer." She paused. "And yet the police are looking at her death as suspicious. Does that mean someone strangled her?" Her face was horrified.

"I think they're trying to figure that out. Did you notice anyone's location during book club or after?"

Pamela shook her head. "Sadly, I'm not very helpful with those details, as I told the police. I did notice Dylan hovering around the refreshments for a bit. I think he was just anxious about being around Margaret after the horrid way she acted about his open mic night. As for me, I left right after we finished. The meeting exhausted me, as it often does. Margaret was always tiresome. I went home, made myself some herbal tea, then turned in early. The police asked me if anyone could confirm that, but I live alone. So I suppose I'm still a suspect."

"Did you know Margaret well outside the club?" asked Sam.

"No, just from the meetings, which was more than enough. Margaret was always . . . " She seemed to catch herself. "This is just my opinion, and of course I didn't know her well. And, I'm no psychiatrist. But she *seemed* like someone who might have had an inferiority complex or something. She was always trying to prove she was better and smarter than everyone else. I wonder what her upbringing was like and if her parents were that way. The thing is, she was a clever, successful woman. She could have been so interesting to converse with. It's really just a pity."

Sam said, "Did you know her from work at all?"

Pamela's brow wrinkled. "You mean from the library? No, I think Margaret had a fairly shabby opinion of the Sunset Ridge library. She preferred her college library. More academic, of course. You could likely tell that she didn't think much of books she termed 'fluff.' Which was basically anything without footnotes or written later than the 1700s."

Sam smiled. "Did Jane Austen qualify as fluff?"

"Oh, Jane was the fluffiest!" Pamela chuckled.

A resident came in on a walker and cheerfully greeted Pamela, who gave her a hug and asked how the resident's physical therapy was going. Then she helpfully directed her toward a new author she'd discovered who wrote women's fiction, the resident's favorite genre.

Sam was about to go look for Nora when the old woman suddenly appeared in the library with Precious, the dog's nails clicking on the linoleum floor.

Nora looked aggrieved about something. The cause of her grievance was revealed when she spluttered to Sam, "Mr. Holloway says Precious has gained weight. Can you imagine? I feed him precisely the recommended portions."

Precious trotted to Pamela with the confidence of a dog who knew he was both handsome and loved. He still wore his argyle sweater vest, which somehow made him look even more distinguished.

"Oh, Pamela! I should have known you'd be here in the library," Nora said warmly. "I was just telling Sam that you volunteer here regularly."

A genuine smile crossed Pamela's face. "Nora, it's good to see you. And Precious, of course." She bent down to greet the pit bull, who accepted her attention with his usual dignity.

"I brought Edith a casserole," Nora said. "Though between you and me, I suspect she shares half of everything I bring with her roommate."

"Most likely," Pamela agreed. She glanced at the clock on the wall. "I should probably wrap up here. I've been organizing donations for a while." She gestured to the cart of books she'd been sorting. "We got three boxes from the library's last sale."

"The residents must love that," said Sam.

"Yes," agreed Nora. "you do such wonderful work here. How many years has it been now?"

"Five," Pamela said. There was a touch of pride in her voice. "Ever since I retired from the county library. It's given me something meaningful to do that also puts me around books again."

"Well, I think it's wonderful of you." Nora checked her watch. "We should let you finish up. I'm sure you have things to do before you head home."

"Actually, I'm done for the day," Pamela looked at the neatly organized cart with satisfaction.

They walked toward the lobby together, making small talk about the retirement home's upcoming holiday party and the new mystery novels that had just arrived. Sam found herself genuinely liking Pamela with her quiet competence, her obvious dedication to the residents, and the way she spoke passionately about books.

They were almost back to the lobby when they heard a child's delighted voice echo down the hallway.

"Precious! Arlo!"

Chapter Twelve

Franklin came racing up, his sandy brown hair sticking up in all directions and his too-big t-shirt flapping. Sam smiled at her young neighbor, who occasionally helped her walk Arlo. He skidded to a stop and immediately dropped to his knees, letting both dogs enthusiastically greet him.

"Franklin," said Nora with evident pleasure. "I didn't know you were here today."

"Mom's doing health checks for the residents," he said, scratching Arlo behind the ears while Precious attempted to climb into his lap, despite her relative size to his lap's size. "She's a nurse, you know. And there's no school because of a teacher workday. Mom told me I could come if I stayed out of the way and brought my homework."

Pamela smiled warmly. "Your mom's a big help over here. How's school going?"

"Good, Ms. Cross. I got an A on my science project."

"That's wonderful," Pamela said. "Your mother must be very proud."

Franklin's mom, Lisa, appeared a moment later, looking harried but smiling. She wore scrubs and carried a blood pressure cuff. "Sorry, everyone. He promised he'd stay in the activity room." She gave her son a pointed look.

"But I heard the dogs," Franklin protested reasonably. "How was I supposed to concentrate on fractions when Arlo and Precious were *right here*?"

"A valid argument," said Nora in complete seriousness.

Sam hid a smile. "Hi, Lisa. How are the health checks going?"

"Good. We're almost done for the day." Lisa checked her watch. "Another thirty minutes and we can head home."

Franklin was now lying flat on the floor. Arlo stood on his chest and licked his face while he giggled. Precious sat beside them like a dignified guardian, his tail thumping against the linoleum.

"Franklin, sweetheart, you need to let them go," Lisa said.

"Can't I just walk them around the building once? Please? I've been doing homework for *hours*."

"It's been forty-five minutes," Lisa said dryly.

"Which is basically hours when it's fractions."

Pamela glanced at her watch. "I should get going anyway. You all enjoy your evening. Keep up the good work in school, Franklin."

"I will, Ms. Cross."

Nora glanced at Sam, who nodded. "Five minutes won't hurt," said Sam. "We're not in a rush."

Franklin scrambled to his feet with the speed only a nine-year-old could manage. He took both leashes with practiced ease. He'd walked Arlo enough times to know the routine. I'll be super careful. And I'll stay on this floor."

"Five minutes," Lisa warned. "Then back to the activity room after you bring the dogs back here."

Pamela said her goodbyes and headed toward the parking lot. They watched Franklin head down the hallway, both dogs trotting happily beside him. Precious's nails clicked importantly on the floor.

"That boy," Lisa said with affection. "He's been asking for a dog since he was four. But it's just too hard with my nursing schedule and the divorce." She shook her head. "Borrowing Arlo sometimes is the compromise."

"He's good with him," Sam said. "Very responsible."

"He is. He takes after you with the organization thing." Lisa smiled. "He color-codes his homework folders. I don't know where he got that from. Certainly not from me or his father."

"Some of us are just born that way," said Sam, returning her smile.

Lisa's radio crackled. "I should get back. Thanks for letting him have a few minutes with the dogs. It'll make the rest of the homework session actually bearable." She headed back down the hallway.

Nora watched her go, then said thoughtfully, "Lisa comes here twice a month. She does wellness checks, medication reviews, that sort of thing. The residents adore her. And Franklin." She paused. "He's a good boy. Franklin reminds me of my grandson at that age. Before he grew up and moved to Seattle and only calls on my birthday."

It was the most personal thing Nora had shared with Sam. She looked at Nora with a new understanding. "You miss him."

"Of course I do. But that's what grandchildren do. They grow up and have their own lives." Nora adjusted her purse with brisk efficiency. "Which is why I adopted Precious. A dog will never move to Seattle and forget to call."

Franklin reappeared, slightly out of breath, the dogs looking pleased at their unexpected walk. "That was the best five minutes ever," he announced, handing the leashes back to Sam and Nora.

"Back to fractions," Nora told him solemnly. "Your future depends on it."

"That's what Mom says." Franklin didn't sound convinced. But he waved goodbye and headed back to the activity room, calling over his shoulder, "Bye, Arlo and Precious."

Sam, Nora, and the dogs walked to Nora's car.

"Well?" Nora asked when they were out of earshot. "Did you learn anything useful from Pamela Cross?"

Sam thought about the tension that had gripped Pamela when Margaret's name came up. "Maybe," Sam said slowly. "She definitely doesn't like talking about Margaret."

"Most people didn't care for Margaret," Nora pointed out, opening the car door. "That doesn't make them murderers."

"No," Sam agreed, helping Arlo into the back seat. "But it's interesting that she claimed not to know Margaret well. Charlotte said Pamela usually helped clean up after meetings. You'd think that would give her more than a passing familiarity with the other members."

Precious jumped into his front seat spot with practiced ease, turning to gaze out the window as if ready to supervise their drive home.

Nora started the engine. "So now we head to the Italian place. You look like you could use a good meal."

"What about the dogs?"

"Hmm?" Nora had a bewildered expression as if she weren't exactly sure whom Sam was referring to. "Oh, you mean Precious and Arlo? It's a nice enough day to sit outside, don't you think? There's plenty of patio seating out there, particularly at this time of the day. Come on. It's not as much fun eating by myself."

The Italian restaurant's patio was nearly empty at this hour, just past the lunch rush and well before the dinner crowd. A server brought water bowls for the dogs, who settled companionably under the table while Sam and Nora studied their menus.

"The chicken piccata is excellent," Nora said. "Though I'm partial to their carbonara."

Sam ordered the piccata, and they fell into an easy conversation about nothing in particular: the upcoming holidays, their neighborhood, and Precious's ongoing weight management program despite his allegedly perfect portions.

"Mr. Holloway at the retirement home suggested more walks," Nora said with a sniff. "As if we don't walk enough already. Precious has a naturally stocky build."

Precious, hearing his name, lifted his noble head from beneath the table. His argyle sweater vest had ridden up slightly on one side. He looked hopefully up, perhaps wondering if he might be given a sample of the menu items once they arrived.

A few minutes later, they were eating their delicious meals. Sam found herself genuinely enjoying the food and the company. Nora had a way of making her laugh with her acerbic observations about Sunset Ridge residents, delivered with just enough affection to keep them from being truly mean-spirited.

"You should come by the house sometime," Nora said as they finished. "I've been meaning to have you over properly. None of this standing on doorsteps business."

"I'd like that," Sam said, surprised to realize she meant it.

As they drove back to the neighborhood, Nora said casually, "I ran into Olivia this morning, on her way out to volunteer at the food pantry. She looked a bit worn out, poor thing. Have you talked to her much since this all started?"

Sam realized with a guilty start that she hadn't spoken with her friend at all. "I should check on her."

"Might be good timing. She mentioned she'd be home all afternoon."

Chapter Thirteen

Olivia answered the door on the second knock, and Sam immediately saw what Nora meant. Her friend looked exhausted, with dark circles under her eyes that makeup couldn't quite conceal. Her auburn hair was pulled back in a messy ponytail, and she wore an oversized cardigan despite the mild weather.

"Sam! Good to see you. I was just making tea. Want some?"

"Sure." Sam followed her into the tidy kitchen.

Olivia went through the motions of tea preparation with automatic precision, but her hands shook slightly as she filled the kettle. Sam waited, sensing her friend needed to get to something in her own time.

Finally, with mugs of chamomile tea in front of them at the small kitchen table, Olivia spoke. "The police came by again yesterday. Chief Hawkins."

Sam's heart sank. "Oh, Olivia." Her friend had really been through the wringer as a suspect in various recent investigations. She seemed to have a habit of being in the wrong place at the wrong time.

"I know." Olivia stared into her mug. "I haven't done anything wrong. This is just routine, of course. They're talking to everyone who was at book club." Her voice caught a little. "But sitting there again, answering questions, and having Hawkins look at me like I might be a murderer was pretty awful." She stopped, wrapping both hands around her mug as if seeking warmth.

"I'm so sorry," Sam said quietly.

"The worst part is, I can see it in the cops' eyes. They know my history. They know I've been involved in similar situations before. That they've had to question me before." Olivia gave a hollow laugh. "I guess once you're connected to murder investigations, you stay connected. Like some kind of horrible recurring character."

"That's not fair to you."

"Fair or not, it's true." Olivia's expression was distant. "Hawkins was professional about it. But I could tell. I'm not just another book club member to them. I'm someone with a track record."

Sam reached across the table and squeezed her friend's hand. "What did they ask you?"

"The usual. Where I was during the meeting, did I notice anything unusual, what was my relationship with Margaret." Olivia set down her mug.

"What did you think of her? Honestly?"

Olivia considered this. "Margaret was difficult. But you already know that. She had strong opinions about everything, and she wasn't shy about sharing them. I felt bad for some of the others. Dylan, especially, after that open mic disaster."

"Did she seem to have problems with anyone specifically?"

"With everyone, really." Olivia frowned. "Although there was something strange about Sofia."

"The grad student?"

"If that's even what she is." Olivia's frown deepened. "She's still a fairly new member. At first, I thought she was just shy, you know? Quiet. And she seemed pleasant. But sometimes, she got this look on her face like she was pained about something. Particularly when Margaret spoke during the meetings."

"Did she have a run-in with Margaret?" Sam asked.

"Maybe. I mean, everyone else did. At any rate, Sofia doesn't speak up much during the meetings. I wonder if that will change now that Margaret is dead."

"Maybe Sofia just doesn't like conflict and wants to avoid it."

"Maybe. Still, it was almost as if she was taking Margaret's actions personally." Olivia wrapped her hands around her mug again. "And there was one moment a couple of meetings ago. Margaret was going on about something. Who even knows what it was. Sofia stared at her with this almost unfathomable expression."

"Anger?"

"No. More like she was grieving," said Olivia. "I've been around enough grief to recognize it." She sighed. "After Dom, I saw that look in the mirror for months. Sympathy for myself, I guess." She gave a short laugh.

Sam felt a pang of sympathy. "I'm sorry."

"It's not like you haven't been through much the same thing," said Olivia.

"Did you mention Sofia to Chief Hawkins?"

Olivia shook her head. "I was too busy trying not to fall apart. Or trying to prove I was innocent, I guess. Besides, what would I even say? Sofia looked sad? That's not exactly evidence of anything. Chief Hawkins would probably laugh in my face. That state police lieutenant would be even worse."

"Did Sofia and Margaret ever interact directly that night?"

"Not that I saw. Sofia mostly stayed quiet during discussions. But she watched Margaret constantly. And when Margaret left the room to visit the restroom at the meeting, Sofia's whole body relaxed. Like she'd been holding her breath."

"What about after book club? Did you see Sofia leave?" asked Sam.

"She left before we did, actually. She said something about an early class the next morning. Which makes sense if she's really a grad student. But I did notice something else. When Margaret was particularly harsh at book club, criticizing the book club selections or something, Sofia whispered something under her breath."

"What did she say?"

"I barely caught it. But it sounded like 'just like her.' Almost like Sofia knew her from somewhere else."

They sat in silence for a moment, the afternoon light slanting through the kitchen window. Outside, a car drove past, its radio briefly audible before fading into the distance.

"I'm probably reading too much into it. Honestly, I'm probably reading too much into *everything*. Maybe I'm desperate to find someone else who's a better suspect than I am. I'm just really tired, Sam." She attempted a smile. "Sorry. You came here to check on me, and I'm dumping all of this on you."

"That's what friends are for," Sam said gently. "And it's going to all turn out fine. You didn't have any motive whatsoever to murder Margaret. There's no evidence because you didn't do it. The police are going to look at everyone else who was at the meeting. I promise you."

Olivia's eyes filled with tears. "Thanks," she whispered. "I needed to hear that.

They finished their tea talking about lighter things like Olivia's volunteer schedule and Sam's plans for Arlo's next agility training.

"I have news," Olivia announced with a smile. She pulled out her phone and showed Sam a picture. "Meet Marmalade. He's twelve, orange, and apparently just wants to sit in sunbeams and purr. The shelter approved my application this morning."

"Oh, he's gorgeous." Sam looked at the photo of the marmalade tabby sprawled across a cat bed. "When do you bring him home?"

"In a few days. I've already bought him three beds, even though I have the feeling he'll probably be camping out on my lap a lot." Olivia's smile dimmed slightly. "It's nice to have something happy to focus on."

By the time Sam left, Olivia looked tired but calmer; the worst of the storm had passed.

Sam pulled away from Olivia's house feeling lighter than she had in days, although her mind was still busy trying to digest everything she'd learned so far.

She wanted to dig deeper, but she also wanted some direction. Maybe someone with investigative experience who knew how to read between the lines of public records.

Sam took out her phone at a red light and texted Aiden. *Free this afternoon? Need your detective brain.*

His response came quickly. *For you? Always. Your place or mine?*

Mine. I'll make coffee.

Thirty minutes later, Aiden sat at her dining room table with his laptop open. Arlo contentedly sprawled across his feet. Sam had her own computer out, along with a legal pad already filling with notes.

"So Sofia Smith," Aiden said, pulling up the Western Carolina University website. "Grad student in what program?"

"She never said specifically. Just 'grad student.'" Sam frowned at her notes. "Which is sort of vague, now that I think about it. Wouldn't you usually say what program you were in? Maybe she's just really private, though."

Aide nodded. "I wonder if she might be a teaching assistant for a professor."

"I think a lot of grad students do that to earn money while they're in school. Maybe she's in the faculty directory?"

They worked in comfortable silence for several minutes, the only sounds were Arlo's occasional snuffling and the click of keys. Sam found herself acutely aware of small things: how Aiden had rolled up his sleeves, showing his forearms. How he'd brought his own coffee mug from home and set it next to hers without comment, like he belonged in her kitchen. How their knees touched under the table and neither of them moved away.

"Hmm," Aiden said, leaning closer to his screen. "I'm not finding a Sofia Smith in the faculty directory. Or in the school's social media."

"Nothing?" Sam frowned.

"Let me try a broader search." He typed quickly. He paused. "Wait. Here's something."

Sam scooted her chair closer to see his screen. Their shoulders pressed together as they both leaned in.

"Is this your Sofia?" he asked. "Sofia Brennan. She graduated with an undergrad degree seven years ago. It looks like she might not have enrolled full time in the program, according to her social media. Her last known address was in Asheville."

"Brennan," Sam said slowly. The name triggered something in her memory. "That's Margaret's last name. Dr. Margaret Brennan."

Aiden turned to look at her, and Sam could see the gold flecks in his brown eyes. "You think they're related?"

"Olivia said Sofia watched Margaret like she was grieving." Sam's mind raced. "What if Sofia is her daughter? Or stepdaughter?"

"That would explain why she joined the book club. I'd have thought a grad student would be too busy to do much outside reading." Aiden was already typing again. "Let me see if I can find any family connections." He turned to look at her. "Nice catch."

"We make a good team."

"Yeah." He smiled. "We really do."

She realized she was still leaning against him, and she didn't want to move.

"Found something," Aiden said, breaking the moment. He clicked on a link. "Here. Margaret Brennan's obituary from the

Sunset Ridge Gazette. It lists survivors." He scrolled down. "Look—'survived by her daughter, Sofia Brennan, of Asheville.'"

"So Sofia might have misled us about being a grad student." Sam pulled her legal pad closer, jotting notes. "But why join your mother's book club under false pretenses? Why not just say who you were?"

"Maybe they were estranged," Aiden suggested. "You said Olivia noticed Sofia looking pained when Margaret spoke."

"Right. It sounds like unresolved family dynamics. But then why go to book club at all?" Sam tapped her pen against the pad. "If you're estranged from your mother, you don't usually seek out her social groups."

"Unless you're trying to reconnect," Aiden said slowly. "Or gather information."

"Or you're checking up on her before you murder her," Sam said.

They sat in silence for a few moments, the implications settling between them.

"I need to talk with her," said Sam.

"Want company?"

Sam nodded. "Definitely. Tomorrow morning? I'll text her and set something up."

"It's a date." Aiden smiled, then seemed to catch himself. "I mean, not a date-date. Just, well."

"I know what you meant." Sam smiled back, feeling warmth spread through her chest. Then, on impulse, she added, "But maybe we could do an actual date sometime soon? Dinner?"

Aiden's expression softened. "I'd really like that."

"Me too." And she meant it. Sitting here with him, researching together, Sam realized she'd stopped second-guessing every moment. She wasn't thinking about her ex-husband or failed marriages, or all the ways relationships could go wrong. She was just thinking about Aiden, and how much she trusted him, and how good it felt to have someone show up every time she asked.

"So," Aiden said, his voice lighter. "Tell me more about what Olivia noticed at book club. The little details you're so good at catching."

Sam launched into a recap of her conversation with Olivia, and they spent the next hour building a profile of Sofia Smith—or Brennan. All her possible motives.

When Aiden left for the night, with plans to meet the next morning for their interview with Sofia, he paused at the door.

"Thank you for calling me," he said. "For letting me help."

"Always," Sam replied, echoing his earlier text. And then, before she could overthink it, she stood on her toes and kissed his cheek." See you tomorrow."

She closed the door and leaned against it, a smile playing on her lips. Arlo trotted over and sat at her feet, looking up at her expectantly.

"Don't look at me like that," Sam told him. "I'm allowed to be happy.

Arlo's tail thumped against the floor in apparent agreement.

Chapter Fourteen

Thankfully, Sam had a better night's sleep than she'd had the night before. By the time she collapsed into bed after Aiden left, she fell into a dead sleep for nearly twelve hours. Twelve much-needed hours after such a long day.

The next morning, Sam sat in her sunroom, Arlo on her lap as she drank her second cup of coffee.

Her phone buzzed with a text from Aiden. *Pick you up in 20 to talk with Sofia?*

Sam texted back to tell him she'd be ready. She gave Arlo an apologetic look. "Sorry, buddy. I'm going to head out with Aiden in a few minutes." She rubbed his soft coat for a couple of minutes before moving to get ready.

Sam supposed they were going to go to the coffeehouse to catch Sofia. She smiled. She was going to be wired after another cup of coffee. Maybe she should get a decaf.

A few minutes later, she climbed into the car as Aiden gave her a warm smile. "Sleep well?" he asked.

"Like a rock."

Aiden drove toward downtown. "How do you think we should approach Sofia this morning?"

"Directly. She's already misrepresented herself to the book club. Dancing around the issue won't help."

"True," said Aiden.

Sam frowned a little. "But then, it does sound like she just lost her mom. We don't know what happened between the two of them, but that must have been hard for Sofia. We'd better tread carefully until we know the exact situation."

Mountain Perk was quiet, but then, it was a Saturday morning. Most people in Sunset Ridge were having a later start. It occurred to Sam that Sofia might not even be working that morning.

But she was. When they walked in, Sofia was behind the counter. When she spotted Sam walking in with Aiden, her face tightened.

Aiden ordered a large coffee, then turned to see what Sam wanted. "I'll have a decaf," she said. Then she added, "Sofia, I was wondering if I could talk with you for a minute. Do you have a break coming up?"

Sofia pressed her lips together. "Give me five minutes."

They sat at a corner table after Sofia got their drinks. A young man came out to take over behind the counter.

"Thanks for talking with us," Sam said as Sofia took a seat with them.

"Did I really have a choice?" Her voice was defensive.

"Sure you did," said Aiden. "But we thought you might want to talk something out before Chief Hawkins comes back with more questions."

Sofia's eyes widened slightly. "What do you mean? More questions about what?"

Sam said in a quiet tone, "The fact you're Sofia Brennan. You were Margaret's daughter, weren't you?"

Sofia took a deep breath. "That's right. But it's not what you think. I was trying to reconcile with my mother. I never wanted any harm to come to her."

"You'd left after book club ended, you said." Sam searched her face. "Did you notice anything else? See anyone else leaving?"

Sofia said, "I didn't really see much. There was just so much tension between my mother and me. I thought that was the reason she stayed behind in the back room of the bookstore. She didn't want any interaction with me." She hesitated. "I think Claire was still in the shop when I left. She'd been talking to Charlotte. And Gerald was heading to his car when I pulled out."

Of course, the problem there was that the murder very likely took place before anyone left the shop. After the poison in Margaret's coffee had taken effect.

Aiden said quietly, "You said you were trying to reconcile with your mom. What happened between the two of you?"

Sofia rubbed her face. "My mom happened." She glanced over at Sam. "You met her. You saw how she was."

Sam said, "I'm guessing she was probably a pretty tough person to grow up with."

"Yeah, you could say that. I mean, my mom was brilliant, but she couldn't turn off the criticism. Not even with her own daughter."

"That must have been hard," said Aiden.

"She pushed me really hard in high school. No grade was ever good enough for her. If I was proud about an A I'd gotten, she'd tell me I should have gotten a 100 on the test instead of a 95." Sofia shrugged as if it hadn't been a big deal, but the hurt was written across her features."

Sam said, "It's especially bad when criticism is coming from a parent. I didn't have the best relationship with my folks, either."

Sofia gave her a curious look. "Are you still in touch with them?"

"Not for a few years. They'll call me, but I don't pick up."

Sofia nodded. "I totally get it. My mom was furious when I didn't get into her alma mater. She thought I'd go to Brown University, the same as she had. When I was rejected, she acted like I'd failed at life."

"So you fell out of touch when you went off to college?" asked Aiden.

"Yep. I decided to take out loans. Well, Mom told me she wouldn't pay for my school since I'd been 'such a disappointment.' At that point, I just took out my loans and stayed at school instead of ever going home. Over the holidays, I stayed with a friend's parents." She shrugged again, but the hurt was still there.

Sam said, "When did you last speak with Margaret? Before you joined book club, I mean."

"Three years ago. I called on her birthday to wish her a happy day. But she lectured me for fifteen minutes about my career choices. I couldn't take it." Sofia took a deep breath. "I like to think I can let that kind of poison just roll off of me, but I can't do it. I guess that's just a flaw I have."

"Not at all," said Sam. "Believe me, I totally get it. I'm the same with my parents. I wish it was different, I really do. But I have to consider my own mental health."

Aiden asked, "What made you decide to join book club? Did you know your mom was a member?"

Sofia nodded. "There was a small write-up in the paper about it. The reporter had gotten a few quotes from members and one of them was my mom. It was supposed to be a piece that helped generate business for Twice-Told Tales after the hurricane had done so much damage. Anyway, I saw that and decided to join." She paused, thinking. "I wanted to see who my mother was when I wasn't around. I wondered if she was different with other people or if she was difficult and critical with everyone."

"What did you find out?" asked Sam.

"That she was just herself. Brilliant and cutting and incapable of holding back." There was sadness in her voice.

Aiden said, "Did your mom recognize you? It sounds like it had been a while since you'd seen each other. You said the last time you talked was on the phone."

"That's right. It had been six or seven years. And no, she didn't seem to recognize me at first." Her tone was bitter. "But then, she didn't really look at me when Charlotte introduced me to the group, and I wasn't using her last name. She acted indifferent."

"But later? She knew who you were then?" asked Sam.

"It took a few weeks. Then I saw her studying me, this sort of flat expression on her face. She didn't look happy to see me.

But she clearly knew who I was." Sofia sighed. "I thought maybe if I could understand my mom better, I could figure out how to talk with her. I wanted to try to bridge that gap between us."

Sam said gently, "You wanted your mother alive."

"Of course I did. I was angry and hurt, but I didn't want her dead. I just wanted her to really see me for once. Maybe to even be proud of me." She gave a short laugh. "Although that might have been asking too much. But our time together was cut short anyway, so I guess I'll never know."

They were quiet for a few moments. Then Sofia continued. "Look, I know how this seems. You're right that it's better for me to figure out how to present this because the police are sure to take it seriously. I lied about who I was. I lied about how I was connected to Margaret. My mom. I just panicked."

Aiden nodded. "It's understandable. Still, it's probably better for you in the long run to tell the police about your connection to Margaret before they find out on their own."

"You're right."

Sam said slowly, "So, the last time we spoke, you mentioned Dylan was someone who might have wanted to murder Margaret."

"That's right. Honestly, he's the one who worried me most. After that open mic disaster and the interview where my mom gave that awful quote, he was totally devastated."

Aiden asked, "So he was more upset than angry?"

"Well, he was both. Definitely more upset at first. His poetry is something he's obviously passionate about. He was embarrassed by what happened. But then, a couple of weeks later, something shifted. Dylan looked furious to me. There was something on his face. It looked like he wanted to kill her. Believe me, I understood. My mother took it way too far."

"Did you ever hear Dylan threaten your mom?" asked Sam.

Sofia shook her head. "Not in so many words. But his body language was pretty clear. I mean, other people weren't happy with my mom either. But his anger was the most visible in the group. And, after all, his humiliation was both public and documented. I wouldn't have thought it possible for him to murder her at first, but after the newspaper article came out, he seemed capable of anything."

Sofia glanced at the clock behind the bar and straightened. "I've got to cut this short. My break's almost over." She looked between Sam and Aiden, her expression still raw from everything she'd revealed. "Thanks for listening. And for not making me feel like a terrible person for lying."

"You were just protecting yourself," said Sam gently.

Sofia managed a small smile. "Maybe. Or maybe I was just a coward who couldn't face telling my mother I wanted to get to know her."

Aiden stood, picking up their empty cups. "For what it's worth, I think it took a lot of courage to go to book club at all."

Sofia's eyes glistened, but she blinked quickly and reached to take the cups from Aiden. "I've got these."

Sam and Aiden made their way out into the bright Saturday morning. The mountain air was crisp, carrying the scent of pine and the first hints of fall.

"That was intense," said Aiden as they reached his car.

"That's an understatement." Sam slid into the passenger seat. "She really thinks Dylan's the threat."

Aiden started the engine but didn't pull out of the parking space immediately. "What did you think?"

Sam glanced up from her phone. "About Dylan?"

"About Sofia. About everything she said."

Sam considered this. "I believe her. I think she wanted to reconnect with Margaret, not murder her. Her grief seemed real." She paused. "But I'm not sure about Dylan being the killer. She's pointing at him because his anger was the most obvious. That doesn't make him a murderer."

"No," Aiden agreed, finally pulling out onto Main Street. "But it does make him someone we need to look at carefully."

"Gerald seemed pretty convinced Sofia was suspicious," Sam mused. "But he might have been deflecting from something he was trying to hide. Everyone's pointing at someone else."

"That's usually how it works." Aiden's voice held a note of dark humor. "Nobody wants to be the prime suspect. So you point at the next most likely person and hope the investigation moves on."

They drove in comfortable silence for a moment, the tree-lined streets of Sunset Ridge passing by the windows. Sam found herself acutely aware of small things again. Like how Aiden had one hand draped casually over the steering wheel, and the way he'd angled the vents so the air didn't blow directly on her, and the faint scent of his soap or cologne.

"So," Aiden said, and there was something different in his tone. Almost nervous. "About tonight."

"Tonight?" Sam felt warmth spread through her chest.

"Dinner. We said dinner." He drummed his fingers on the steering wheel. "And I've been looking at restaurant menus online. Which is ridiculous because I already know all the restaurants in town. After all, Sunset Ridge isn't a huge place." He gave a wry smile. "But I've been thinking about our dinner a lot. Like what I might order. Is going to a fancy place going to make things too serious? Should I just stick with a burger?" He winced. "I'm making this weird, aren't I?"

"Not at all," she said, a smile curling at her lips. "But you might be overthinking it."

"I mean, it doesn't have to be a whole thing," Aiden said quickly. "We can just order pizza at my place if you'd rather keep it casual."

"Aiden."

He stopped, glancing over at her uncertainly in a way that was somehow endearing.

"Where did you want to originally take me?"

He relaxed slightly. "There's this place in town. Ember & Oak. It's not fancy. I mean, it's nice, but it's not upscale." He tried again. "The food's really good. Local ingredients, the whole farm-to-table kind of thing. They do this trout with herbs that's amazing. And they have a patio with string lights if the weather holds."

Sam felt something tighten pleasantly in her chest. He'd clearly been really thinking about this. "That sounds perfect."

"Really?" He looked genuinely pleased. "I was worried that it might not be . . . well, you've probably been to much fancier restaurants than anything Sunset Ridge has to offer."

Sam said, "That's not really what I'm looking for. I moved here for a reason. I'm not looking for fancy."

"Right. Good point." Aiden cleared his throat. "So, seven? I could pick you up around six-thirty?"

"Perfect." Then, because she couldn't resist teasing him a little, "Are you nervous?"

"About dinner? No. Maybe. A little." He shot her a rueful smile. "It's been a while since I've done the actual date thing. Usually we're just researching murder suspects together. Acting like partners on the force."

"To be fair, that's been most of our relationship so far."

Aiden said, "True. But I'd like to have one meal where we don't discuss poisoning methods or blackmail motives."

Sam laughed. "I'll try to control myself."

They pulled up in front of her house, the historic brick façade looking warm and welcoming in the late morning sun. Aiden put the car in park but made no move to rush her out.

"Thanks," Sam said. "For coming with me this morning to talk to Sofia. And for the coffee. For everything." She gestured vaguely.

"Of course. That's what partners do."

The word hung between them. Partners. Not just in investigation, but maybe in other things, too.

Sam reached for the door handle, then paused. "Thinking back to Sofia. I want to believe her. But she's been lying about who she is the whole time. How do we know she's telling the truth now?"

Aiden was quiet for a moment, his fingers drumming lightly on the steering wheel. "We don't. Not completely. But her story makes sense. Her grief sounded real to me. And pointing at Dylan might not be just a way to deflect attention from herself.

Everyone who's nervous points at the most obviously angry person."

"True." Sam sighed. "I just feel like I'm missing something. Like there's a piece that doesn't quite fit."

"Then we'll keep digging until it does." He smiled at her.

Sam climbed out of the car, then leaned back in through the open door. "See you at six-thirty?"

"Six-thirty."

She closed the door and watched him drive away, a smile still playing on her lips.

Chapter Fifteen

Sam had eaten a sandwich and a handful of nuts for lunch when her phone rang. She saw it was Charlotte. "Hi there. How's everything going?"

"Oh, it's okay. Sorry, are you busy right now? Am I interrupting your lunch?"

Sam said, "Not at all. I've just finished."

"Good. I'm at the shop, of course, and I just found Margaret's tote bag. She'd left it here after the meeting. I wasn't sure whose bag it was, so I started going through it to see if I could figure it out. Anyway, do you mind coming by? I wanted to run something past you."

"Sure," said Sam. She frowned. "Why wouldn't the police have taken that as evidence? I thought the whole bookstore was treated like a crime scene."

"That's the truth," said Charlotte wryly. "But there's no name on the outside or anything. The police would have looked in the bag and just noticed a bunch of papers related to book club. They probably thought it was mine and left it behind."

"I'll be right there," Sam said, hanging up. She gave Arlo a rueful look. "I'm going to have to give you a walk and some cuddles later to make up for being gone so much today." She let him out to use the bathroom, gave him a treat, and headed off for the bookshop.

She was glad to see Charlotte had opened the shop at last. It must have been a tough balance between wanting to respect Margaret's loss of life and the financial considerations involved in having the shop open.

"Thanks for coming," Charlotte said with a smile.

"Of course! I see you've opened back up."

"I have, but it's still quiet now. Let's head back to the back room."

Once back there, Charlotte pointed out a canvas bag before walking over to pick it up. "So, it's full of book club stuff, of course. There's a couple of book selections from past months with Margaret's notes in them."

Sam hesitated. "I mean, should we wear gloves or anything? I guess it doesn't have evidence on it, though, probably. It's just Margaret's belongings."

Charlotte popped herself on the forehead. "Wow, I didn't even think about that, even after I realized it must be Margaret's bag. Now my prints are all over it. How about I just pull out some plastic gloves for you, just in case. We can tell the cops about this bag after we take another look."

Sam felt a little better about going through the materials with the latex gloves on. She opened one of the book club selections, which looked like a fantasy. Margaret's marginalia was very critical of the book. It was interesting to see how critical she could be even when she was writing personal notes to herself. There was a red folder in the bag, too, that said 'book club' on it.

Sam opened up the folder. It looked like membership lists, meeting schedules, and then, oddly, printed emails.

"Why would Margaret have printed out her emails?" asked Sam. "Was she sharing them with other people? She could have just forwarded them."

Charlotte shook her head. "Margaret always said she didn't trust technology. She'd delete emails after she printed them out. She thought she might get hacked or something. Anyway, take a look."

Sam pulled out a sheaf of printed emails. The one on top caught her eye. It was from geraldine.hartwell22 at a gmail account. It regarded dues collection from the club members. And Margaret had written in black ink *Geraldine = Gerald.*

Sam stared at the email. "Geraldine Hartwell. Gerald?"

Charlotte nodded slowly. The silence was heavy in the back room.

"So Gerald has a double life?"

"No, nothing like what you're thinking," said Charlotte. "But it's a pen name. Something he didn't want anyone to know about."

"But you know. When did you find out? When you read the email?"

Charlotte said tiredly, "I've known for months. I'm a bookstore owner. I read romances and know the authors. I've seen him researching Regency-era details in a book at the shop. Then one day he accidentally wrote me an email from that address, asking me to order a book. After that, I put it all together. But I didn't realize Margaret had figured it out."

"Clearly, he was still logged into his pen name email account by accident," said Sam.

"Right. He was just sending out the reminder. He must have forgotten he was still logged in as Geraldine."

Sam said, "Did anyone else notice?"

"No one said a word about it. I thought no one else had paid any attention. I should have known Margaret wouldn't let something like that pass by her."

"But she didn't say anything to him during the next club meeting?" asked Sam.

"No. Although she had this expression on her face like a cat who'd eaten cream. Smug. But then, she could look smug regardless. She did spend more time bashing romances and romance readers than usual after that, but that was pretty typical Margaret behavior. I didn't know until I came across this printed email that she knew." Charlotte's expression was miserable. "Do you think Margaret was trying to blackmail Gerald or something?"

"Is that something you could see Margaret doing?"

Charlotte gave a helpless shrug. "I'm not sure. She seemed to have plenty of money. But then, she kept saying she wanted to go on a trip to Dublin, Ireland and see the different literary sites there. So who knows? Or maybe she blackmailed him to just make Gerald suffer. That's a possibility. She's capable of it, for sure."

"But you never asked Gerald about his pen name?"

"No," said Charlotte, looking defeated. "I figured it was his business. Lots of authors use pen names. I thought if he'd wanted us to know, he'd tell us. But now I'm feeling guilty. Maybe if I'd been paying more attention, Margaret would still be alive."

"You're thinking Gerald murdered her to keep her quiet? And to keep her from taking more of his money, if she was blackmailing him?"

Charlotte sighed again. "When you put it that way, it sounds like a lot. I mean, obviously Gerald didn't want information about his romance writing getting out, for whatever reason. But it's not exactly a motive for killing someone, is it? If he were being blackmailed, though, it makes a little more sense."

"He could have been furious at Margaret for putting him in the position to begin with."

"I guess," said Charlotte. "I just can't see him being violent. Secretive and probably anxious, yes. But not violent."

Sam liked Gerald. She didn't want him to be guilty. But the motive was definitely there. "Do you have one of Gerald's books in stock?"

Charlotte nodded and headed out of the back room. A few moments later, she returned with a beautiful historical romance. "He's with a major publisher, too." She hesitated. "Sometimes, male authors are worried about having their work accepted if they use their real identity. Maybe Gerald was worried about that, too. That his books wouldn't be as popular if readers knew he wasn't a woman."

Sam said slowly, "I think I should talk to him." She looked at her watch. "The bank is open on Saturday for a few hours, I think, right?"

"That's right. I feel bad about exposing his secret, though."

Sam said, "I know. But someone might have died and he's free to kill again, if that's the case."

"You can't just approach someone who might have committed a murder, Sam."

"I'm going to see him at work. It's still his lunch break, and he sits outside the bank there. It's totally public, but also private enough to have a talk," said Sam. "And I'll text Aiden, too, to let him know. Maybe he can meet me there. But you need to call the police to tell them what you found. They must have thought it was just your book club records and didn't realize the significance of it." She took out her phone and took a picture of the printed email. Then she texted it to Aiden with a quick note about heading to the bank to speak to Gerald.

Charlotte was still fretting. "I should go with you."

"This is the first day the bookshop is open again. You might get a few customers."

Charlotte said, "I can flip the sign to 'closed' for thirty minutes or so."

"I'll be fine. Besides, Gerald might be more honest one-to-one."

Charlotte shook her head. "I wish I'd told someone when I first figured out who Gerald was. Maybe this never would have happened."

"You were respecting his privacy. That's not wrong." She gave Charlotte a quick hug, promising to keep her informed. Then she headed out of the store.

Chapter Sixteen

A few minutes later, she pulled up at the bank. Mountain Trust kept Saturday hours from 10:00—3:00, which was something the big chains had given up on. Gerald, if he kept his same lunch break, was probably already outside on that bench with his book and brown bag lunch.

Sam checked to see if she'd gotten a text reply from Aiden, but he hadn't responded yet. So Sam walked around the side of the bank to the wooden exterior stairs leading from the upper parking lot to the employee patio area on the back of the building. Then she headed down the worn but sturdy stairs to the concrete patio. Gerald was sitting on a stone bench near the bottom of the stairs, facing away from her. From what Sam could tell from the back, he was reading a book. He had a thermos and sandwich wrapper sitting beside him on the bench. Sam took a deep breath.

"Gerald?" she asked.

Gerald swiftly looked behind him, nearly dropping his book. "Sam. What are you doing here?"

"Sorry, I didn't mean to startle you. I wanted to talk to you about Geraldine." Sam walked around Gerald to another bench that faced him.

Gerald froze. "You know about that?"

Sam nodded. "And Margaret did too, right?"

"She found out because I used the wrong email account one day. But it's not how it looks, Sam. Listen, you can't tell anybody about this. The cops will get the wrong idea."

Sam said, "They're going to find out anyway. They're investigating everybody. And it's not just the local police, but the state police, too. Wouldn't it be better to tell them before they find out?"

Gerald slumped. "I'm not sure that's a good idea. They're just going to take that and run with it. They won't even look at anyone else."

Sam said, "How long have you been writing historical romances?"

"It's been five or six years." He shook his head. "I can't believe this is happening."

"You should be proud of your success. You've got a major publisher. And Charlotte says your books are very popular."

Gerald frowned. "Charlotte knows, too?"

Sam wanted to make that clear. She didn't think Gerald would come after her, but she still didn't want him to think he could eliminate her and remove the only person who knew his secret. "That's right."

Gerald said, "Look, I don't want anyone to know about this. The bank has a strict no-outside-employment policy. I don't know if it extends to being a novelist, but I don't want to find out."

"Tell me what happened with Margaret."

Gerald rubbed his temples as if they throbbed. "Margaret was very snide about it. Well, you met her. You know exactly how she could be. She demanded $500 a month from me or else she'd tell the bank and everybody else if I didn't pay." He shook his head. "I've been bleeding my savings dry. I know how this all looks, but I didn't do a thing to Margaret."

"But it must have been a huge relief when she died."

He blew out a sigh. "Sure. But that made me feel guilty too, even though I had nothing to do with it. I was terrified of her, but I didn't wish any harm on her. I kept thinking she must have had a tough upbringing or that something awful must have happened to Margaret to make her the way she was. I felt sorry for her, in a way. I didn't want to be her target, though. She was always giving me these knowing looks. Like she was about to spill the beans and tell everybody at any time. And writing is the only thing I do that's mine and mine alone."

It felt like he was telling the truth. But he looked guilty at the same time. Maybe it was just because he felt relieved at Margaret's death.

"You're not going to the police, are you?" he asked.

"I have to," said Sam. "You have a motive."

"But others have a motive, too. Everyone saw how upset Dylan was after his open mic night."

Sam asked, "Was there anyone else who might have wanted to harm Margaret?"

Gerald hesitated. He looked clearly uncomfortable, as if he didn't want to say anything.

"Gerald, if it's not you, then who?"

In a low voice, Gerald said, "Claire."

"Claire Mills?" Sam frowned in surprise.

"I really shouldn't say anything. She's my friend. We talk about writing all the time."

Sam asked, "Did Claire know about your romance writing?"

"She knew I was working on something, but not what it was. I told her it was a historical novel, not a historical romance. Anyway, Margaret just destroyed her. She really did."

"What do you mean?" asked Sam. She knew this was about Margaret's critique of Claire's book, but she wanted to hear Gerald's take on it.

"Claire's been working on a manuscript for years. She summoned up the courage to ask Margaret what she thought about it." He shook his head. "I told her not to do it. I said even if Margaret loved it, she wouldn't give Claire any praise. Margaret was someone who ripped people down, not built them up. But Claire really wanted feedback."

"Why didn't she just get you to read it?"

"She did," said Gerald. "I thought it was great. But Claire thought she couldn't really get an honest opinion from me because we were friends. She figured Margaret would be honest. Then Margaret just eviscerated the manuscript. Her criticism broke Claire. She stopped coming to meetings for a couple of months."

Sam shook her head. "That must have been rough on her."

"Claire kept working on the manuscript. Really obsessively, actually. Like she couldn't let go of what Margaret said. She told her she'd never be published. That she should give up on writing entirely. But it was always Claire's dream." Gerald rubbed his hand over his face. "I feel so bad telling you this. I don't think Claire could have hurt anyone."

"But she does have motive." Sam stood. "I'd better run. I'll let you finish your lunch. Thanks for talking to me."

He nodded miserably as Sam left. When she got to the top of the wooden stairs, she turned back to see Gerald sitting on the bench, his head in his hands.

As soon as Sam got back home, she texted Charlotte to see if she'd let Chief Hawkins know and to tell her she'd safely returned from her talk with Gerald. She hadn't wanted to tell Gerald that it would be Charlotte making the call to the police instead of her. She didn't like the idea of Charlotte being in any danger. Charlotte texted her back to say that she'd just done it. She asked how Gerald had been, and Sam filled her in as Arlo greeted her with enthusiastic tail wags.

Then she sat down with her notes again, carefully recording Gerald's secret and how Margaret had discovered it. That she'd been blackmailing him monthly.

Nearly an hour passed when her phone rang. It was Aiden, his voice tight and urgent. "Sam. Where are you? Are you okay?"

"At home. Why? What happened?"

He breathed a sigh of relief before saying, "Right before I got your text, my neighbor, Elsie had a medical issue. She doesn't drive anymore, so I took her to urgent care. By the time I was able to get my phone back out and saw all the cops at the bank, it just scared me."

"Cops at the bank? What happened?"

"It's Gerald Parker. He's dead."

Chapter Seventeen

Sam's stomach dropped. "No. No, I just talked to him."

"I asked my cop friend what was going on at the bank, and he told me. When Gerald didn't come out from his lunch break, a member of the staff came looking for him. He was dead at the bottom of the employee stairs leading down to the patio."

"No. Those back stairs?" She felt sick thinking of it. Had Gerald been so upset by their conversation that he'd slipped and fell?

"That's right."

Sam asked, "Does it look like an accident? When I left him an hour ago, he was sitting outside having his lunch."

"My friend said it looked like a suspicious death. They're treating it like a homicide for the time being."

Sam's voice shook. "I can't believe this. It must have happened right after I left."

"I'm coming to see you."

"Aiden—"

"I'm already in the car. Be there in five minutes."

Sam sat, her phone still in her hand, feeling numb. Arlo put his head on her knee like he knew something was wrong.

Her thoughts were racing. She'd confronted Gerald. Upset him. Then he went up those stairs alone, shaken by what she'd told him. Had he missed a step and fallen down those steep stairs? Had someone met him at the top of the stairs, shoved him while he was so distracted, and killed him? If so, didn't that mean that there was something Gerald knew that the killer didn't want revealed? Why hadn't he said something?

She'd exposed Gerald, made him vulnerable. If he had been murdered, the killer might have seen Gerald speaking with her. They'd have realized Gerald was talking, and they wouldn't have known what it was about.

Arlo started barking, and Sam hurried to the door, peering out before she opened it. Aiden came in, took one look at Sam's face and drew her carefully into his arms. She rested a moment there, feeling his strength and calm before pulling away. "The police will want to talk to me."

Aiden nodded. "I'll drive you over to the bank."

They walked to his car and climbed in. Sam blew out a deep breath. "I feel like this is all my fault."

"You didn't kill him, Sam. Only one person is responsible for that. I'm just sorry I didn't get your text message until it was too late. I'd have been at the bank with you."

Sam shook her head. "I backed Gerald into a corner. Someone must have known he was vulnerable. They might have figured he was exposing them."

"You were just trying to find out the truth."

On the way over, Sam filled in Aiden, her story sounding disjointed and broken to her own ears. By the time they reached the bank, the area was cordoned off with police tape. An ambulance and other police vehicles were at the scene. Sam saw the cops speaking with the bank employees, who all looked shaken up.

Hawkins approached, wearing a grim expression and looking frustrated. "Ms. Prescott. I understand you were speaking with Gerald Parker a little over an hour ago."

Sam cleared her throat before answering. "That's right. He was sitting on that bench." She pointed. "I was on that one. Gerald was eating his lunch."

"And what did you discuss?"

Sam took a deep breath. Aiden gave her an encouraging look. "His secret. He was a romance novelist who wrote under the pen name of Geraldine Hartwell. Margaret was blackmailing him."

Hawkins gave a curt nod. "Charlotte Webb called to let us know that just a short while ago."

"What happened? Do you know?"

Hawkins looked at her as if weighing how much he wanted to share. "The bank manager found him at the bottom of those stairs. He fell from the top of them to the bottom and didn't survive his injuries."

"Fell or was pushed?"

"We won't know for sure until the medical examiner takes a look. But given the circumstances and a couple of other things, we're treating his death as suspicious. I think someone wanted him dead, the same as Margaret Brennan." He stared steadily at Sam. "And I think you should watch your step, Ms. Prescott. The killer, if there was one in this case, might well have seen you meeting with the victim. You might be the next target."

Sam nodded, feeling a cold chill run up her spine. Aiden looked at her with worried eyes.

Hawkins continued. "You need to tell me exactly what your conversation entailed."

And so she did. From the point where she told Gerald she knew his pen name, to the point where he discussed his feelings about Margaret's knowledge, to the blackmail, to his pointing at both Dylan and, reluctantly, to his friend Claire Mills.

"Claire Mills," said Hawkins, jotting a note down in a small notebook. "What did Gerald Parker say about her?"

"He said she had motive. Claire was a writer, too. Gerald said she didn't know that he wrote romance novels, but she was aware he was working on a book. He said Claire was devastated when Margaret heavily criticized her manuscript. Margaret had basically told her to give up on writing because she'd never make it."

"We'll check it out," said Hawkins. "But Ms. Prescott, this is a double homicide now. There's an active killer. You need to step back."

Sam said quietly, "Gerald talked to me right before he died. I'm already involved."

Hawkins gave her a frustrated look. But he didn't say anything more.

A black sedan pulled up, and a state policeman stepped out. Sam recognized him from another investigation. He was in his late-40s, tall, with graying temples and sharp eyes. Lieutenant Phillips.

"Chief," he said to Hawkins. "What do we have?"

"Second homicide. At least, it appears to be. Same social circle as the first victim."

Phillips took control naturally. "Let's make sure the scene is completely secured. And I want statements from everyone who was at this bank today."

He turned to Sam as Hawkins stepped away to check the scene. A woman in her mid-50s walked up and straight to Gerald's body. Looking at how she was carefully studying him, Sam figured she must be the medical examiner. Then Phillips took her aside, farther from Aiden, and had Sam repeat everything she'd just told Hawkins. The blackmail, how she'd spoken to Gerald at lunch, how he'd admitted to being Geraldine Hartwell.

Phillips took notes as she talked, asking questions intermittently. He seemed, as usual, methodical and thorough.

"How did Gerald seem? Did he appear desperate? Like someone who might have thrown himself down the stairs?"

Sam shook her head, but her stomach fell at the thought. Had she pushed Gerald to kill himself? "He seemed scared and shaken up. But that's it."

"Who knew that you were meeting him?" asked the lieutenant.

Sam hesitated. Charlotte had, of course. And Aiden. Although neither of them had any reason to murder Margaret or Gerald. Still, she mentioned them.

Phillips nodded. "Anyone else?"

Sam shook her head again.

The middle-aged woman who'd been examining Gerald's body called to Phillips. He briskly excused himself and stepped aside to speak to her. Sam waited. Neither of them seemed to realize she was still within earshot.

"I'm Dr. Sarah Chen, the county medical examiner," said the woman. After Phillips had introduced himself, he said, "What do you think?"

"His injuries are consistent with a fall from that height. He's exhibiting a broken neck and head trauma."

Phillips said, "Does it appear to be an accident? Suicide? Homicide?"

"There's bruising on his upper arms consistent with being grabbed or pushed. There are also defensive wounds on his hands. I noticed scraped knuckles and a broken fingernail."

"So he fought back," said Phillips.

"Briefly. Someone pushed him. He tried to stop himself, but couldn't. He fell backward down the stairs."

Phillips turned and seemed to remember Sam was there. She said, "Did you need me to stay to finish our conversation?"

"We're done," said Phillips curtly. "But I'll be in touch."

Aiden and Sam headed up to the parking area. "You okay?" asked Aiden.

"I'm okay. But I feel awful about what happened to Gerald. I did overhear the medical examiner saying Gerald's death was definitely murder, so I won't worry I drove him to kill himself. But still." She paused. "Who could have done this? Obviously, Gerald wasn't the one who murdered Margaret. So who did?"

Aiden shook his head. "Gerald must have known more than he was letting on."

"Or the killer thought he did. Gerald specifically mentioned Dylan and Claire. But was it someone else? Why wouldn't he have let the police know?"

Aiden said, "Maybe he wasn't sure. Maybe he'd seen something that didn't quite click, but wanted to check it out for himself before making any allegations."

Sam sighed, leaning against his car. "I feel like I shouldn't have left him alone. He was obviously a target."

"He was at a bank. Generally, that's a pretty safe place. And he was a target because he knew something. Not because of anything you did." Aiden's face was concerned. "Do you want me to come in with you after I drop you back home? Talk this out?"

Sam shook her head. "Thanks, but no. I think I need some time to just decompress. Maybe get distracted by Arlo."

"Arlo sounds like a great distraction. But call me if you change your mind. I don't have anything going on right now." Aiden carefully didn't mention the supper they'd planned that night. He probably wasn't sure it was something they should still do. Sam, at this point, felt so depleted that she wasn't sure either.

Chapter Eighteen

Minutes later, Sam was back home. Arlo greeted her enthusiastically, nuzzling her leg as she walked inside.

Her phone rang. Sam glanced at the screen, smiling when she saw Ginny's name there. Ginny was the president of the local agility club that she and Arlo belonged to. Arlo loved the exercise and the interaction with the other dogs there. And Sam liked all the club members. "Hi Ginny," she said.

"Hey there! Pixie is losing her mind with boredom, so I decided to make an impromptu Saturday afternoon agility gathering. Are you and Arlo in?"

Pixie was Ginny's Jack Russell, and she had just about as much energy as Ginny did, which was saying something. At first, Sam didn't think she felt like she could rise to the occasion. Then she realized it might be just what she needed. And it would be good for Arlo, too. He was smiling his doggy grin at her, tail wagging as if he somehow knew who was on the other end of the phone.

"Sure. Right now?"

"Come on by!" said Ginny. "I've already called some of the others. See you soon."

It wasn't long before Arlo and Sam joined the group in the golden light of the late afternoon. The dogs were playing freely on the field. Dave's border collie, Rocket, was fruitlessly trying to herd everyone while Ziggy, the whippet, was making huge loops on the field. Arlo was trying to keep up on his short legs. Sam felt herself laughing, feeling the tension slowly releasing from her body.

No one was talking about murder, either. They were talking about the types of dog food they were giving their animals, about agility training and how their dogs were doing with it, and Sam's young friend, Franklin's, agility course that he'd made behind the community center.

Lucy, Ziggy's owner, approached Sam with a couple of water bottles and Ziggy at her heels. "Sam, do you have a minute? I need to bounce something off you."

"Sure, no problem, Lucy. What's up?"

She leaned forward. "I hope you don't mind me being nosy. But I heard you were at Charlotte's bookstore when Margaret was found. I'm sorry. Was she a friend of yours?"

Sam thought wryly that she should have known she couldn't completely stay away from talk about the murders. She still hadn't gotten used to living in a small town and how quickly gossip could spread. "No, Margaret was a new acquaintance of mine. We were in book club together. But it was still very shocking."

Lucy nodded, looking sober. "I bet it was. It's hard to believe something like that could happen in Sunset Ridge. And in Twice-Told Tales, of all places." She paused. "I didn't know Margaret, but I'd kind of gotten a bad impression of her. Was she always hard to get along with?"

"She could be, I think. Margaret had sort of a prickly personality from what I could tell."

Lucy said, "I saw Margaret recently, as a matter of fact."

"When did you see her?"

"It was just a day or two before she died. I was walking Ziggy through downtown after we'd hit the trails. Margaret was arguing with Claire Mills. Do you know her?"

Sam said, "Yes, she's our book club president." She frowned. "Could you hear what they were arguing over?"

"Not much. Of course, I was trying to act like I wasn't listening in. Margaret said something about Claire should be thankful for her honesty. But Claire didn't look thankful at all. She was crying. Like, a lot." Lucy made a face. "I was wondering if I should say something to the police. I feel like I'm the town busybody. I know I had to talk to the cops about something during that last investigation, too."

"You're just someone who's really observant and who covers a lot of ground with those long walks of yours. It's not like you're trying to impose yourself in the middle of other people's business."

"Well, it sure feels that way," said Lucy wryly. "Anyway, I thought I'd bounce that off you. See what you thought. I guess I'll give a statement to the police. I just hate doing it because Claire has always been really nice to me. I feel like I'm throwing her under the bus."

"No, she's already on the police radar as a member of book club. And I think they'd appreciate getting a little more perspective on who had issues with Margaret."

Lucy nodded, looking relieved. "Okay. Thanks, Sam. I feel better about it." She stood up. "Come on, Ziggy. Let's see if you can keep up with Rocket."

The whippet bounded around her, and Sam watched them rejoin the group. Across the field, Ginny was orchestrating what looked like an impromptu game of chase, with Pixie yapping orders at dogs three times her size.

"She's trying to herd Rocket," Dave called out, laughing. "A Jack Russell herding a border collie. I've seen everything now."

"Pixie's got aspirations," said Ginny. "She's management material."

Sam felt the last of the tension drain from her shoulders as she watched Arlo flop down in the grass, tongue lolling, clearly exhausted but happy. He looked cute but funny with his short legs sticking out at odd angles.

"Arlo's done," Dave observed, walking over. "That's his 'I gave it my all' pose."

"He did give it his all," Sam agreed. "About fifteen minutes of it."

"Hey, that's impressive for a dog who's basically half basset hound, half fluff."

Sam laughed, feeling lighter than she had in days. This was exactly what she'd needed; dogs being ridiculous, friends making terrible jokes, and an hour where murder wasn't the main topic of conversation.

Well, mostly not the main topic.

By the time Sam and Arlo made it home, the sun was setting and Arlo was moving at approximately half his normal speed. He'd given everything to keep up with the athletic dogs and was now paying the price.

"I know, buddy," Sam said, unlocking the front door. "You're not built for marathon running. But you had fun, right?"

Arlo's tail gave one tired wag before he trotted straight to his bed and collapsed.

Sam smiled as she headed to the kitchen. Her appetite was starting to return. But were she and Aiden still going out to supper? It had been a really heavy afternoon for both of them. Her stomach, though, made protesting noises. Maybe a small snack would be the best course of action until she knew for sure.

But the fates weren't interested in Sam getting to eat. The doorbell rang. Arlo lifted his head from his bed, gave a half-hearted "woof," then put his head back down. Clearly, he was off duty.

Through the front window, Sam saw a familiar silhouette on her porch. And an even more familiar pit bull shape beside it.

She opened the door to find Nora holding a covered dish, Precious straining at the leash. The pit bull was wearing what appeared to be a burgundy smoking jacket with black satin lapels.

"Wellness check," said Nora crisply, sweeping past Sam before she could respond. "I hear you were on the scene at the bank. I brought soup."

"Nora, I . . ."

"Don't Nora me. I saw your car pull up a while back, and I figured you'd be standing there staring at your refrigerator like it might spontaneously generate a meal."

It was very close to what she'd been doing. Nora could be astoundingly perceptive.

"Now, you don't have to eat it right this second. But it's here for you when you want it." Nora briskly walked over to the fridge and stuck it in.

Precious trotted over to Arlo's bed. Arlo opened one eye, assessed the situation, and apparently decided Precious wasn't worth getting up for. Precious settled down beside him, smoking jacket and all.

"Those two," Nora said, shaking her head. "Precious has been moping around all day. I think he missed his friend." She turned to face Sam with gleaming eyes. "Now. Gerald Parker. At the bank."

"You know everything that happens in this town, don't you?"

"Not everything. But I'll get there. You look exhausted. What happened?" Nora peered at her. "I'm right, aren't I? You look peaked. You haven't eaten, have you?"

Sam's stomach chose that moment to growl, answering for her.

"That's what I thought. I can heat up that soup right now. It'll be perfect with some buttery crackers."

Sam said, "Maybe in a few minutes, but thanks. On a totally different topic, any updates on the online dating front since the last time we talked about it?"

"I met someone." Nora's smile was cautiously optimistic. "He doesn't seem as awful as the other guy I met. This one's name is Harold. He's a retired accountant, and he's actually normal. We had coffee together this morning, and he hasn't once tried to explain cryptocurrency to me or tell me I remind him of his ex-wife."

"Hey, that's wonderful, Nora!"

"We're taking it slow. Very slow. But I think I might actually like this one. We shall see." Nora paused. "Though I have to say, after everything that's happened with Margaret and Gerald, it's made me appreciate that life's too short to waste time on people who don't make you happy. Which reminds me. When are you going to do something about that handsome teacher of yours?"

Sam felt her cheeks warm. "I'm not sure what you mean."

"Sure you don't." Nora's eyes twinkled.

The doorbell rang again.

Nora's eyebrows shot up, and her expression transformed into delighted nosiness. "Expecting someone?"

"Not really." It wasn't yet time for Aiden to come by, if he was coming by at all. Sam headed for the door, wondering who else might show up on her porch.

She opened the door to find Aiden standing there with several takeout bags, looking slightly sheepish.

"I figured you probably hadn't eaten," he said. "I brought some takeout from the Thai place. I thought maybe tonight wasn't the best night for us to go out to dinner." He paused, spotting Nora in the background, her face infused with pure matchmaking satisfaction.

"Well, hello, Aiden," purred Nora.

Aiden flushed a little. "I just thought Sam might need something to eat."

"Great minds think alike." Nora gathered Precious with suspicious speed. "I was just leaving. You two enjoy your . . . dinner." Her eyes gleamed at Sam.

At the door, she turned to give Sam a stage whisper. "He brought Thai food. Keep this one." Then, she and Precious exited with a flourish, leaving them alone.

AIDEN GAVE A LOPSIDED smile. "Should I apologize for chasing off Nora?"

"Are you kidding? She'll be gossiping about this for weeks. You've made her day."

Aiden made himself at home in her kitchen, bringing out plates, napkins, and pouring ice water. He hesitated. "Would you like some wine? I feel silly offering you your own wine, but I forgot to bring some."

"You know, a glass of wine would actually be perfect right now. I'll grab it."

Aiden said, "No, I've got it. Just relax wherever you want us to eat. I'll bring it all in."

Sam walked into the living room, feeling slightly chilled, maybe from tiredness. Her stomach growled again, complaining about its emptiness more audibly. She turned on the gas fireplace as Aiden made several trips into the room with food and drinks.

She gave him a rueful look. "I do sometimes eat at the table, I promise. But I don't think I feel up to it tonight."

"I'm sure you don't." He sat next to her on the long sofa. Arlo, perking up from his bed for just a moment, decided to hop up between them, falling promptly asleep again as they smiled at each other.

Aiden glanced over at the book on the coffee table. "Still working through *Middlemarch*?"

Sam looked at the book, covered with color-coded sticky tabs. "I'm on page 387 now."

Aiden studied the setup on the coffee table. The book, three different colored pens, and a small stack of index cards with character names. "You've added index cards since we talked about it."

"They help me track the relationships."

Aiden's smile was gentle. "You're amazing, you know that?"

"I'm compulsive."

"You're thorough. But still totally amazing."

They ate their food in comfortable silence, watching the fire. Then Aiden talked lightly about other things: the essays he needed to grade soon, an upcoming parent conference, how he'd gotten his yard ready for winter. Sam listened, nodding, as she quickly ate her food. Neither of them wanted to talk about the day.

After they'd finished, Aiden cleaned up the kitchen, loading the dishes into the dishwasher. Then he said, "I'm going to head on out. What do you think about moving our dinner to tomorrow night? Our real dinner."

"I'd like that."

Aiden's hand found hers, and he gave it a gentle squeeze. Then he gave her a brief kiss on the forehead. "Get some sleep. See you tomorrow."

Sam watched him from the window as he walked to his car.

Chapter Nineteen

Sam slept like a rock. Arlo was similarly out after his agility club exertions, sleeping hard right next to her. The next morning, she woke before dawn and prepared to head to church. She found the services seemed to really reset her for the week ahead. She left Arlo still dozing on her bed.

Sunset Ridge Presbyterian Church was a beautiful old church with a traditional white exterior, a tall steeple, and red double doors. Sam decided to go to the adult Sunday school class and head home before the service. She walked over to the fellowship hall downstairs. The class's teacher was a retired professor who favored the Socratic discussion style. Right now, they were studying the book of Ecclesiastes. It was a convivial class with about 12 to 15 regulars.

As the class started, she saw Claire quietly hurrying in, looking exhausted and drawn. She looked across the room, saw Sam there and nodded a greeting. Sam gave her a smile in return.

The professor, Marvin, started talking about "what has been will be again . . . that there was nothing new under the sun." He discussed cycles of human behavior, the patterns that repeat themselves.

Marvin said, "The Hebrew word here, *yesh*, implies 'already exists.' Not that *nothing* can be new, but that human experience keeps circling back."

A woman in her sixties said, "My grandma used to say 'different day, same foolishness.'"

There was laughter around the room.

A younger member of the class said, "But doesn't that make everything kind of meaningless? If we're just repeating cycles?"

"I think that's the tension we need to sit with. Observe the patterns, but don't despair of them."

The class continued as Sam glanced over at Claire from time to time. She was usually a lot more animated in Sunday school, asking questions and contributing to the discussion. When the class ended, Claire just quietly gathered her things.

Before Sam could come up with an excuse to speak with her, she walked over to Sam.

"Hey there," she said. "Do you want to grab a coffee? I think I'm going to skip the service today."

"Sure. I'll meet you over there."

A few minutes later, they met at Mountain Perk. It was late-morning now and moderately busy at the coffeehouse. They both ordered coffee and muffins and sat down at a booth in the corner. Sofia wasn't there, so must have had the day off.

Claire gave her a sympathetic look. "I heard you'd spoken to Gerald shortly before he died."

Sam nodded. "I'm afraid so. I'm sorry. I know the two of you were friends."

The words made Claire choke up for a few moments. Sam waited until Claire felt she could speak again. "Thanks. I feel bad for you, too. First Margaret, then Gerald. I don't know what's going on. Is our whole club getting targeted? I couldn't even sleep last night, worrying about it."

Sam said carefully, "I don't think that's the case. I think whoever murdered Margaret is scared. Maybe they thought Gerald knew something. That he saw something. They got rid of him in order to protect themselves."

Claire took a deep, steadying breath. "Right. You're right. I've just gotten all wound up about it. You know how everything seems different at night. It's easy to start imagining things. Maybe if I actually *got* some sleep, I wouldn't be this paranoid."

"It's only natural," said Sam gently. "These were two people you saw regularly."

Claire nodded. "Did the police talk to you about Gerald?"

"They did. I'd seen him right before he died." Now Sam was the one swallowing and trying to maintain her composure. "I was talking to him about his writing."

Claire gave a small smile. "He and I talked a lot about writing. He was trying to work on a historical novel of some kind. We gave each other tips we'd read online."

"Did you hear that he was already published?" asked Sam carefully.

"What? No. He was? Did he publish it himself?"

Sam shook her head. "He'd actually published quite a few books through a major publisher. Historical romances." She studied Claire's reaction. But there was no mistaking the shock that crossed her features.

"You're kidding. I had no idea." Claire sat back in her chair, looking stunned. "But why wouldn't he tell me about that?"

"It sounded like he was trying to keep it under his hat. He had a woman's pen name. Maybe he thought he wouldn't be taken seriously by readers if he wrote as a man. Or maybe he just wanted to keep it private. But it sounds like he was pretty successful."

Claire just shook her head quietly. "He was really supportive of my writing. But when I suggested we critique each other's work, he told me he wasn't ready to do that. I guess that's why."

Sam said, "I had something else I wanted to ask you. You know how people in Sunset Ridge talk."

Claire now looked apprehensive. "You can say that again."

"I spoke with someone who mentioned seeing you have an argument with Margaret shortly before her death. Outside of Mountain Perk, actually."

Claire closed her eyes. "I wondered if anyone noticed."

"Can you tell me what happened? And you should probably mention it to the police, too. If I know about it, the police are sure to find out soon." Sam left out the part where Lucy said she was going to report it directly.

Claire took another deep breath. "It was just Margaret being Margaret. Trying to make everyone feel small."

"Was it about that critique she gave you for your manuscript?"

Claire shook her head. "I mean, that was bad enough, obviously. I really wanted an objective opinion of my manuscript before I started sending it off. Gerald had already told me no, like I mentioned. So I asked Margaret." She winced, remembering. "I don't know what I was thinking. I should have handed it to

Charlotte, instead. She's read a ton of books and should know if something needs more work or not."

Sam said, "I'm guessing you thought to ask Margaret because she was used to marking students' papers. She'd get right to the point about what wasn't working."

"Right. That's true. I was a little worried that Charlotte wouldn't want to make me feel bad. That she'd try to pump me up by telling me what a great job I'd done. But I wanted some honest criticism." She sighed. "I got that in spades from Margaret. But our argument was about more than that. Margaret had some publishing connections."

Sam frowned. "Did she?"

"From her academic career. She'd published herself, you know. You pretty much have to in order to get tenure at colleges. Anyway, she loved going to conferences and that kind of thing. She knew a few people. A few months ago, I told Margaret I was going to submit my manuscript to Red Mountain Books. It's this small independent press in Western North Carolina."

Sam asked, "This was after Margaret had given you ideas for revision?"

"After she tore it apart, you mean. It gutted me, but she had valid points. I worked night and day on those revisions. Anyway, Margaret offered to send an email along with the book to her contact over there. I was delighted. I couldn't believe Margaret was actually being helpful for once."

Sam said slowly, "Let me guess. She totally torpedoed your submission."

"Bingo. I got a rejection from the publisher just a week later. It was a kind rejection, but definitely a no. The editor sent along Margaret's notes, as a 'courtesy.' So I knew what to work on." Claire's voice was bitter. "She'd questioned my genre understanding, called my work 'amateur,' and said I 'lacked the capacity for sustained narrative.'" Claire's face was red and blotchy, and she looked as if she might start crying again.

"I'm so sorry," said Sam gently. "I hope you'll try to submit the manuscript again to another publisher. It sounds like Margaret just wanted to sabotage you. Maybe she was jealous."

Claire shrugged. "I don't know. I'm not sure I want to open myself back up again to rejection. It's pretty tough."

"You'd confronted Margaret about it? Outside the coffee shop?"

"That's right," said Claire. "I knew her coffee routine, so I waited for her. When she came up, I asked for an explanation. Why she'd done it. She said she wanted to save them from publishing trash."

"What happened then?"

"I yelled at her," said Claire. "I mean, I knew how Margaret was. But it was hard to believe she'd gone the extra mile to ruin my chances with Red Mountain. She just looked so smug. So self-satisfied. I let her have it. But I *didn't* kill her. I would never do anything violent. I was furious and devastated and definitely angry. But after that one big tirade, I was done." She shook her head. "I went home and considered quitting writing. My husband talked me down. And later, Gerald did. He told me just what you did. That Margaret might be jealous."

They were quiet for a few moments, Sam drinking her coffee and Claire taking a bite of her muffin. Then Claire said quietly, "Can you tell me more about what happened to Gerald?"

"I wanted to talk with him about him having a pen name. It sounded like Margaret had found out."

Claire rolled her eyes. "Oh, that would have been a nightmare. Margaret would have dangled that over his head. Or she'd have made all kinds of cutting comments during book club meetings while looking at him." She stopped. "Is that what you were thinking? That Gerald murdered Margaret to stop her from revealing his secret?"

"It was something I was worried about." She paused. "Clearly, that doesn't seem to be the case."

Claire frowned. "Well, it doesn't look like Gerald killed her. But now that I think about it, Margaret did keep making these sorts of smug references to 'secret identities' and 'secrets' during book club. Like she was baiting someone. I didn't know what the point was at the time. But I guess she was blackmailing him, in a way. Maybe not extorting real money from him, but emotional blackmail, for sure." She shook her head. "That woman was a piece of work."

"Do you have any ideas about who might be behind this?"

Claire considered this. "I hate to think anybody in our club had anything to do with either death. I'm the club president, you know and its biggest booster. Even with Margaret, I've always thought the club was a wonderfully supportive environment."

"The last time we spoke, you thought maybe Gerald could have done it."

Claire winced at this. "Yeah. And he was my friend," she said bitterly. "Obviously, I was wrong. If I had to pick someone, I guess I'd say Pamela or Sofia. I've seen them look at Margaret.

I could tell neither of them liked her much. But like I said, I can't picture either of them murdering anybody." She gave a bitter laugh. "It sounds like I had the bigger motive, didn't I? But I didn't do it. And I would never have hurt Gerald. He was my biggest cheerleader besides my husband." She said quietly, "How did he die? Do you think he suffered?"

"No. No, I think it was quick." She didn't mention how he'd died.

Claire nodded. "Okay. I know it was yesterday afternoon. I was out running errands, which isn't helpful at all. I'm sure the police, whenever they talk to me again, are going to think that's not much of an alibi."

"Just tell the police exactly what you told me. The truth is your best defense."

Chapter Twenty

After she and Claire finished up at the coffee shop, Sam headed back home. She stood in her kitchen, staring at nothing in particular. Margaret hadn't been a good person in a lot of ways. But she hadn't deserved what had happened to her. She felt terrible for Claire, too. She hoped she'd somehow find the confidence to keep going and submit her story to another publisher.

She should update her notebook and review her suspect list. She needed to think through everything she'd learned.

Instead, she opened her pantry.

Arlo, who'd been napping in a patch of sunlight, lifted his head with interest.

"Don't look at me like that," Sam told him. "I'm not stress-eating. I'm stress-organizing."

She pulled out her label maker, the one Nora had given her for Christmas with a note that said, "I know you, dear" and surveyed the chaos before her.

The pantry had been bothering her for weeks. Items shoved wherever they fit. Spices in no particular order. Cans facing random directions. Her Type-A soul had been quietly screaming about it, but there'd always been something else that needed to be done.

Like solve murders.

But right now, she needed something she could actually control. She pulled everything out, creating organized piles on the kitchen counter. Baking supplies, canned goods, pastas and grains, snacks. Spices alphabetized, because of course they would be.

Arlo wandered over to supervise, sniffing at a can of green beans that had rolled off the counter and toward his water bowl.

"That's a vegetable, buddy. You won't like it."

She wiped down the pantry shelves, measured the spaces, and started creating labels. Each one that she pressed into place felt like a small victory.

Sam was so in the zone that she jumped when her phone rang. It was Nora.

"I hope you're relaxing," said Nora briskly.

Sam hesitated.

"You're organizing things, aren't you?"

"Guilty as charged," admitted Sam. "But that's something that's relaxing to me. And I'm about to have a bowl of your soup."

"Good girl," said Nora. "Although I'm not totally sure about organizing being relaxing. Try to put your feet up before your date. You know your man doesn't care if your pantry is alphabetized."

"How do you know I have a date?"

Nora sniffed. "I know everything. Have fun."

And with that, the omniscient Nora hung up.

Sam shook her head, smiling despite everything. She finished the pantry, stepped back, and felt something in her chest unclench slightly. Everything had a place. Everything was labeled. And at least in this one small area, chaos had been vanquished in a minor way.

That evening, Sam had changed outfits three times before Arlo had given her a look that clearly communicated *just pick something already*. She'd settled on dark jeans and a soft blue sweater that Olivia once said brought out her eyes.

The doorbell rang at exactly six o'clock. Punctual. She appreciated that.

Aiden stood on her porch holding a bottle of wine and wearing a slightly nervous smile that made her heart do some complicated acrobatics. He'd traded his usual teacher wear for dark slacks and a charcoal button-down with the sleeves rolled to his forearms.

"Hi," he said.

"Hi." She stepped back to let him in. "You didn't have to bring wine."

"I wanted to." He handed her the bottle, which was a nice Pinot Noir, not the cheap grocery store kind. "And I should probably confess that Nora ambushed me at the store and offered very firm opinions about what I should buy."

Sam laughed. "Of course she did. You realize she's going to interrogate you about this later."

"I'm counting on it. I need someone to tell me if I'm doing this right."

Sam took his arm. "You're doing fine so far."

Arlo appeared, immediately asking for some love. Aiden crouched down to greet him properly. He produced a dog treat from his pocket like a magician.

"You came prepared."

"I've learned." He stood, his eyes meeting hers with warmth that made her suddenly hyperaware of how close they were standing. "So, an actual date night. No interruptions. No murders to discuss."

"Well, about that."

He grinned at her. "Maybe we can have just the one night where we're not detectives?"

Sam smiled back at him. "It's a deal."

They drove to a small Italian place on the edge of town. It was the kind of restaurant Sam had passed a hundred times but never tried. The inside had white tablecloths, soft lighting, and the smell of garlic and fresh bread that made her stomach growl despite the nerves she had. She reminded herself it was just Aiden. But she wanted everything to go well.

"I've been wanting to bring you here," Aiden said as they were seated at a corner table. "It's family-owned. The grandmother still makes the pasta by hand every morning."

"How did you find this place?"

Aiden said, "One of the cops I was working with years ago couldn't believe I was just eating sandwiches or cereal for supper every night." He held up his hand, laughing. "I promise I don't do that anymore. This was when I was still young and dumb. Anyway, he apparently thought I needed an intervention. He told me about this place. I'd come once a week for takeout. It was good food that didn't break the bank. And I've been coming here ever since."

"Someone decided to intervene in your eating habits? That's very Sunset Ridge."

"It is." He opened the menu.

"What do you recommend?"

"Everything. But if you like seafood, the linguine with clams is incredible. If you want something heartier, the osso buco." He paused. "Or we could get a few dishes and share? Fair warning, though, that I'm terrible about sharing dessert."

"Noted." She closed her menu. "Let's share. I want to try everything."

They ordered linguine, osso buco, and a Caesar salad to start. Aiden ordered a wine that made the waiter nod approvingly.

"So," Aiden said once they were alone again. "Tell me something that has nothing to do with book clubs or suspicious deaths."

Sam thought while she tore off a piece of the warm bread that had appeared. "I'm thinking about getting Arlo into therapy dog certification."

"Really?"

"Ginny mentioned it at agility. Apparently, he has the temperament for it. He's calm, loves people, and doesn't get reactive." She buttered her bread. "I thought we could volunteer at the senior center. Or maybe the library for reading programs."

"That's perfect for him. And for you." Aiden took a sip of water. "You like helping people."

"Is that a nice way of saying I'm nosy?"

"It's the accurate way of saying you care." His expression turned serious. "There's a difference in being nosy and being invested. You're definitely the latter."

"Even when it gets me mixed up in murder investigations?"

"Even then." He reached across the table, his fingers brushing hers. "Though I'd be lying if I said I didn't worry."

The waiter arrived with their salad and wine, giving Sam a moment to process. When they were alone again, she met Aiden's eyes.

"Worry about what?"

"About you being in danger. About you being the last person to talk to Gerald before someone killed him. About you asking questions that make a murderer nervous." He traced patterns on the tablecloth with his finger. "I know you're going to keep investigating. I'm not asking you to stop. I'm just asking you to be careful. And to let me help when I can."

Sam said ruefully. "I'm not great at asking for help."

"I know." He smiled. "But I'm pretty good at offering it anyway."

Their entrees arrived. The pasta was fragrant with white wine and garlic, the osso buco was falling off the bone. They sampled both dishes.

"This is incredible," Sam said after her first bite of the linguine.

"Right?" Aiden looked pleased. "That's the grandmother's recipe. She won't share it with anyone. Her son's been trying to get it out of her for twenty years."

They ate and talked, the conversation flowing easily from teaching stories to books to Sam's complicated relationship with her parents.

"They weren't neglectful," Sam said, twirling pasta on her fork. "Just distracted. They were very passionate about their work. Both of them were artists. But they were less passionate about things like parent-teacher conferences and regular meals."

"Is that why you're so organized now?"

"Probably," said Sam. "Someone had to make sure we had groceries and that bills got paid. I was making lists by age seven. They were color-coded by nine."

"Is it your way of keeping chaos at bay?"

Sam paused, her fork halfway to her mouth. "That's surprisingly insightful."

"Former detective. We're trained to notice patterns." He reached across the table, his hand covering hers. "But you know what else I've noticed? You're happiest when you're helping people, not just organizing things. It seems to be your purpose."

"When did you get so good at reading me?" asked Sam.

"I've been paying attention." His thumb traced circles on the back of her hand. "Someone had to."

The simple honesty made her chest tighten. She turned her hand over, lacing her fingers through. "Thank you," she said quietly."

"For what?"

"For being patient. For not pushing. For bringing me here and understanding."

"Sam." His voice was soft. "That's just being here for you. That's what this is."

They finished dinner and ordered the tiramisu despite Aiden's warning about not sharing dessert (they shared it anyway). Then they lingered over some coffee until the restaurant began to empty around them.

"I should probably get you home," Aiden said reluctantly. "Even though I don't want to."

"I don't want you to, either."

They drove back through the quiet streets of Sunset Ridge. In the neighborhood, they passed Nora's house on the way. It was all lit up from the outside and inside. "She's probably watching from her window right now," said Sam wryly.

"Definitely."

When they pulled up to Sam's house, she could see Arlo's face pressed against the window, tail wagging.

"Can I walk you to your door?"

"I'd like that," said Sam.

They stood on her porch, the night air cool but not uncomfortable. Through the window, Arlo had started doing his welcome-home dance.

"I had a really good time tonight," Sam said.

"Me too." Aiden's hand came up to cup her cheek. "Can we do this again? Soon? Maybe without the cloud of double homicide hanging over us?"

"I'd like that. Though, given my track record, I can't promise no dead bodies."

"Fair enough." He smiled, then gently kissed her. Soft and sweet and full of promise.

When they broke apart, both slightly breathless, Sam leaned her forehead against his. "You should probably go before Nora comes over to investigate."

"Probably." But he didn't move. "Sam? Please be careful tomorrow when you're investigating. I'll be back at school, of course, but call me if anything feels off."

"Promise."

He kissed her once more, then stepped back reluctantly. She watched him walk to his car, waiting until he'd pulled away before going inside. Arlo greeted her with enthusiastic snuffles and circles.

Her phone buzzed immediately with a text.

It was Nora, naturally. *He's a keeper. Don't mess this up.*

Sam smiled, texting back: *Good night, Nora.*

Lock your door. Murderer still out there.

Already done.

She got ready for bed and fell asleep thinking not about suspects and motives, but about Aiden's smile and the way his hand felt in hers.

Chapter Twenty-One

Sam had finished her usual morning routine when Charlotte called her.

"Everything okay?" asked Sam.

"Yes. This is becoming a pattern, isn't it? I'm sorry for bothering you. Am I interrupting your breakfast?"

"No, no. I'm all done with that. What's going on?" asked Sam.

"I haven't gotten around to calling the police yet about Margaret's tote bag," said Charlotte. "I know. I should have done it right away. But I had another delivery truck come in, then I had a bunch of chatty customers, then my mom called me and there was something I needed to help her with. Anyway, I went back into the bag."

"You found something else?" Sam thought back to when she was at the shop. She'd felt like they'd really gone through it. But then she realized that as soon as she'd seen Margaret's printed email from Gerald/Geraldine, she'd stopped searching through everything.

"That's right. Do you mind running by? I hate doing this over the phone."

"No problem. I'll be there in a few minutes."

As good as her word, Sam was back in the shop just ten minutes later. Charlotte gave her a rueful look. "Sorry again. I just figured I'd give the bag another quick look before I called the cops. I didn't really think I'd find anything else in there, but I think I did."

Charlotte's hands were gloved, and she handed Sam another pair. "Just because the police might dust for fingerprints or something." Then she handed Sam some neatly-typed pages.

Sam skimmed one of them. "I'm not sure I'm getting the full context of these. It sounds like Margaret, for sure. She's talking about 'academic circles' and 'old betrayals.' People who 'can't handle competition.'"

"I know," said Charlotte. "This looks to be part of her memoir draft, from what I can tell."

"Memoir or tell-all?" muttered Sam. "She's not happy with somebody."

"That's what I thought, too. I wish we had more pages. These might even be from her outline, not the draft. There was one other part there, too. She said something about some people couldn't handle 'being shown their limitations.'"

Sam said slowly, "Who do we think she was talking about?"

"It could be anyone Margaret hurt through the years. There's a letter in that stack, too. From a publisher, it looks like."

Sam sifted through them until she found the letter. She glanced at the letterhead. It was the same publisher that Claire had contacted for her own book. Sam read part of the letter out loud. "Regarding your memoir, we've attempted to contact the relevant parties mentioned in chapters four and seven for comment. Please confirm you've secured necessary releases." Sam looked over at Charlotte. "Who would need to be contacted?"

"I guess anyone she wrote about. If it's potentially libelous. I mean, that's a small press. They wouldn't be able to handle major lawsuits."

Sam said, "Do you think it's about Dylan? That he couldn't handle being 'shown his limitations?'"

"Maybe. Or maybe Claire? She was very upset about Margaret's feedback. Could it be her?"

Sam said, "Maybe. But I don't understand what she means by 'academic circles' unless it's her contacts in publishing. Or the bit about 'competition.'"

Charlotte made a face. "I guess it's not very helpful after all."

"I think the papers are giving us information, but we don't have enough background to understand it. I'm guessing the police probably have the rest of her memoir, so they might have more ideas. Margaret must have kept it at her house."

Charlotte sighed. "And now I'm going to have to call them and tell them they missed Margaret's tote bag." She paused. "Actually, I might just drop it by there, myself. I can close the shop for a few minutes and run it by the station. I hate to have police cars outside the bookstore again. It can't be good for business. What are you doing now?"

Sam thought it through. She usually had a game plan for her day at the very start, but Charlotte's call had interrupted that process. "Dylan works at the community center, right?"

Charlotte nodded.

"I might run by there and see if he's over there and available for a quick chat. It's a nice public place to meet up with him, just in case. I can say I'm there getting pamphlets for their activities. Then I might run by and help Olivia out at the food pantry. She usually volunteers today."

Charlotte said, "See you later, Sam. And thanks."

The Sunset Ridge Community Center occupied a sturdy brick and wood building on the edge of downtown, its wide front porch dotted with rocking chairs that usually hosted retirees. This morning, the parking lot was only half-full. The weekday crowd of senior exercise classes and yoga for moms hadn't yet arrived.

Sam pulled into a spot near the entrance and walked into the building. She'd been there dozens of times for various town meetings and community events, but had never really paid attention to the layout. The main entrance opened into a large multipurpose room that could be divided with accordion partitions. To the right, a hallway led to smaller rooms used for classes and workshops. To the left, administrative offices and a small library tucked into a corner.

Dylan's workshops would be in one of those classroom spaces if he were there. The lobby smelled faintly of coffee and the distinctive scent of whatever industrial cleaner they used on the linoleum floors. A bulletin board near the entrance advertised everything from yoga to council meetings. She scanned it quickly and saw a flyer for 'Creative Writing Workshops with Dylan Morrison, MFA.'

So, Dylan had a Master of Fine Arts. She'd forgotten that, if she'd ever known in the first place. Could he have been in those 'academic circles' Margaret was talking about? Could he have been a teaching assistant for her?

Sam could hear voices from the classroom area. She made her way down the corridor, her footsteps echoing slightly on the polished floor. She peered inside one classroom and saw Dylan there. His dark curly hair looked like it hadn't been combed that morning, and he wore jeans and a faded band T-shirt. Even from behind, she could see the tension in his shoulders. A couple of adult students were coming her way with notebooks in their hands, heading out of the class.

Dylan didn't turn around, so Sam knocked lightly on the doorframe. "Dylan?"

He turned quickly, almost dropping the folder he was holding. When he saw her, surprise flickered across his features, followed quickly by wariness.

"Sam." He set the folder down carefully. "I didn't expect to see you here."

"I hope I'm not interrupting," she said, stepping into the room and gesturing at the pamphlets on the table. "I wanted to pick up some information about the workshops. I thought I might run into you here."

The wariness in his expression didn't quite fade, but he nodded. "Sure. We've got information on everything right here. You're interested in doing some creative writing? Poetry?"

"Maybe. Or I might share it with a friend of mine who could be interested."

Dylan nodded. "There's no judgment here. It's supposed to be a fun class that can help you explore your creativity. I'd love to have you or your friend sign up."

"I like the idea of a no-judgment zone. It sounds very supportive."

Dylan said in a bitter voice, "Yeah, that's what we're aiming for. There are places that don't have that. It can make it really tough on your confidence, especially when you're just starting out. I hate to say it, but book club just wasn't that way."

"It seemed like Margaret had a lot of strong opinions."

"Yes. On everything," said Dylan. "But things should be better now. Aside from her, it was a very supportive environment. And you need that kind of support and encouragement, whether you're exploring books or your own writing."

Sam said carefully, "I understood Margaret was writing too, so you'd think she'd understand. A memoir, wasn't it?"

Dylan frowned. "How did you find out about that? What did you hear?"

"Not much. Charlotte found some memoir pages in some of Margaret's things that she'd accidentally left at the shop. They're with the police now." At least, Sam hoped they were. Especially considering the kind of reaction the mention of them provoked in Dylan.

Dylan went pale. "With the police? What did the pages say? Did Charlotte tell you? Did they mention me?"

"I don't think the pages were very specific. What's wrong, Dylan?" Sam edged closer to the classroom door in case she needed to make a quick exit.

He noticed Sam moving her hand to her pocket to pull out her phone. He raised his hands, trying to look nonthreatening. "I'm sorry. Sorry, Sam." He plopped down into a chair and buried his face in his hands. "What a mess," he muttered.

Sam kept holding her phone but sat nearby in a chair. "What's going on? Is there something Margaret knew about you? Something she was planning on exposing? If there is," she added gently, "it's probably a good idea to let the police know. They're sure to find out, anyway. That way you can get ahead of it."

Dylan nodded, his head still in his hands. "Right. I know." He took a deep breath. "I don't have the MFA I said I had."

"I see." If he didn't have the master's degree, he lost a lot of credibility, especially considering he was teaching courses at the community center.

Dylan said, "I'll lose my job here. That's how I got the workshop gigs. I told them I had a graduate degree. I can't believe this is happening."

"And Margaret found out? How?"

Dylan's laugh was bitter again. "How did she find *anything* out? She stuck her nose into everything. I guess she must have taken it upon herself to do some poking around and see if I had the degree. She threatened to expose me."

"How? Was she going to put it in her memoir?"

Dylan said, "Who knows? She decided to just torture me by telling me she was going to tell people and then didn't do it. I didn't know if she was going to call up the community center or tell people by word of mouth. Or maybe write about it in her memoir. I had no idea. I've been terrified for weeks."

They were quiet for a few moments as Sam tried to absorb the new information and Dylan tried to get control of his emotions. He finally said, "You realize how guilty this is going to make me look to the cops. They're going to think that I killed Margaret because she was going to expose me as a fraud. Because that's what I am, a fraud. But I'm not a killer. I was relieved when she died, of course. That makes me feel awful. But I didn't murder her."

"And Gerald?"

Dylan said, "Of *course* I didn't murder Gerald. I can't believe he's dead. It's like I'm stuck in this nightmare that won't end." He paused. "You're the one who found Gerald, aren't you?"

"No. But I'd spoken to him right before he died."

Dylan shook his head. "I'm guessing that makes you a suspect, too."

"The police aren't really happy about my proximity to both victims. I found Margaret, of course. And then I'd had that contact with Gerald shortly before his murder."

Dylan said, "I can't believe anyone would kill Gerald. He was such a great guy. He was super-creative, too. I thought he'd make a great author."

Sam wouldn't spread Gerald's secret further. Claire knew, but that was different; she'd been his friend.

Dylan was quiet for a few moments. "There was someone else who wasn't happy about Margaret's memoir. Pamela."

"She wasn't?"

Dylan nodded. "She kept asking Margaret what she'd written. Margaret just smiled and said, 'The truth.' Pamela looked kind of sick when she said that."

What could Pamela have been worried about? A retired librarian, volunteering at a retirement home? It seemed unlikely Margaret and Pamela's paths would cross.

Dylan said, "I'm going to head back home now." It was a pointed remark.

"Of course. I'm sorry."

Dylan headed out quickly, with Sam several paces behind.

Chapter Twenty-Two

Sam pulled into the food pantry parking lot and spotted Olivia's Honda. She was glad she wasn't the only one who'd shown up today. Plus, after their last conversation, she wanted to check on her friend. Olivia had seemed shaken by the police questioning her.

Inside, Olivia was hunched over a donation box, organizing cans by type. She looked up and smiled. "Oh, good. Reinforcements."

"I couldn't let you have all the fun," Sam said, grabbing a box cutter.

They chatted about minor things as they organized cans and boxes into categories for shelving. Sam felt herself getting into the rhythm of the work.

"I'm glad you're here," said Olivia after about ten minutes of small talk. "I've been meaning to check back in with you."

"Same. How are you doing?" Sam dropped her voice, although no one was around to overhear them. "Have the police been back to visit after Gerald's death?"

Olivia nodded, but didn't look as anxious as she had before. "They have. But you're right; this is all routine for them. They're just coming back around to interview everyone in book club for a second time because there was another murder." She shook her head. "I'm really sorry about Gerald. He was a great guy."

"He seemed to be," said Sam.

Olivia said, "Are *you* doing okay? I heard you'd spoken with Gerald right before he died."

Sam looked rueful. "News in Sunset Ridge always travels fast. But that's right. I'd caught up with him at the bank. I'm sure I look a lot more suspicious to the police than you do at this point."

Olivia grinned. "You probably do, because I have an alibi for Gerald's death. I was here at the food pantry the whole time. I filled in for another volunteer who couldn't make it."

"Excellent! Glad to hear it. That takes you totally out of the frame."

Olivia said, "Do you have any idea on how the investigation is going? Are the police getting any closer to figuring out who's done it? Because it sure seems like they're not, considering the fact the killer just murdered again."

"I'm not really sure. They're obviously not confiding in me. But I've found out a couple of tidbits."

Olivia raised her eyebrows. "What?"

Sam looked around again to make sure they were alone. "Dylan doesn't actually have a master's degree."

"You're kidding." Olivia's eyes opened wide. "But he's teaching classes and workshops with MFA in his credentials." Then she paused. "Are you thinking Margaret found out?"

"Does that seem likely to you?"

Olivia sighed. "It sure does. I always got the feeling that Margaret had too much time on her hands. Some people step easily into retirement. But it didn't seem like a good fit for Margaret. I can see her getting involved in other people's business out of total boredom."

"Do you think it's possible Dylan could have murdered Margaret to keep her quiet?"

Olivia said, "I struggle over thinking *anybody* in book club could have done it. But somebody obviously did. How did you find out?"

Sam filled her in. Olivia gave a low whistle. "That's a lot. How did Dylan react to being confronted about it?"

"Honestly, he seemed more frightened than guilty to me," said Sam slowly. "But then, I don't really know him. It means he could lose his teaching job at the community center. And he wouldn't want the public embarrassment again once everyone finds out he lied about his credentials."

"No. Not after what happened when Margaret made that comment in the newspaper about his open mic night." She quietly sorted cans for a few moments before saying, "Dylan is very passionate about what he does. He loves writing. He loves poetry. I think he probably spends more time at Charlotte's bookstore than any of the rest of us do. But it sounds like however Margaret died, it was calculated, right? It wasn't a spur-of-the-moment thing?"

Sam said, "Right. It must have been planned in advance."

"I just don't see it. Not Dylan. He's an impulsive guy, so I could imagine him striking out in the heat of the moment. But I can't picture him cold-bloodedly murdering someone."

Sam said, "I found out something else, too. Sofia is Margaret's daughter."

Olivia's jaw dropped almost comically. "You're kidding me."

"Nope. She and Margaret were obviously estranged."

Olivia said, "So why was Sofia there at book club? Was she trying to harass Margaret somehow?"

"It sounded like she wanted to connect with her again. She hadn't spent time with her since she'd left for college."

Olivia said, "And she really *is* in a grad program? As opposed to Dylan?"

"She seems to be, yes. Aiden found her mentioned online as Sofia Brennan."

"Ah." Olivia was quiet again for a few moments, processing everything. "But if she was trying to make up with her mom, killing her sounds like a weird way to go about it."

"Agreed."

Olivia said, "Oh, that reminds me. There's going to be a memorial service for Margaret tomorrow. I got an email from Charlotte."

"Thanks for letting me know. Since I left Charlotte earlier, I haven't had the chance to check my emails. Is Charlotte the one putting it on? I'd gotten the impression she wanted to do something to mark Margaret's death."

"It's actually a niece of Margaret's, apparently. She's come into town to settle her aunt's affairs and wanted to hold a small service. Charlotte sounded a little worried in the email that no one would show up. It's at ten tomorrow morning at the Sunrise Chapel. Are you able to make it?" asked Olivia.

"Absolutely. I don't have anything set on my calendar for to-morrow. I didn't really know Margaret, but I want to support Charlotte. And Margaret's niece, too. It would be awful to hold a service and not have anyone show up. Surely Margaret's former co-workers at the college will be there, though."

Olivia said, "I'm not sure about that. I saw the niece had posted something on Margaret's social media about the service. But who knows if her colleagues will come. Can you imagine working with Margaret? She was tough enough to handle in a club setting. She must have been a nightmare at department meetings at the university."

"True. But maybe some of them will show. I'd be interested in talking to them."

Olivia smiled at her, the old twinkle in her eye. "You mean pumping information out of them?"

"That too," admitted Sam.

"So you've got information on Sofia and Dylan. Gerald is dead. Who's left? Pamela and Claire?"

"I did visit Pamela with Nora at the retirement home where Pamela volunteers."

"Oh, that must have been quite a visit."

Sam grinned at her. "Precious and Arlo were there, too. And Franklin."

Olivia laughed at the mental image. "Classic. Were you able to find out any information, or was it just a total zoo?"

"It's not as bad as I made it sound. Precious and Nora were mostly out of the way, visiting a resident there. Anyway, Pamela clearly wasn't wild about Margaret. I found that out mostly from other people I talked to. She seemed nervous about Margaret's memoir, from what I gathered. As far as Claire goes, she felt betrayed by Margaret."

Olivia frowned. "Because of the way Margaret criticized her manuscript? The critique she gave her?"

"It was more than that. I mean, that was bad enough. But Margaret had apparently told her she'd help her out by sending a note to one of her contacts at the publisher Claire was querying."

Olivia winced. "Oh no. I didn't realize Claire was that naïve. Ugh. What did Margaret do?"

"Apparently, she wrote a scathing review of the manuscript. The publisher didn't end up accepting the book. It devastated Claire."

"Of course it did." said Olivia. She shook her head. "Margaret was a bully in a lot of ways. I'm sorry for what happened to her, but it doesn't excuse her behavior."

Sam murmured agreement, but could sense Olivia's discomfort with the topic. They fell into an easy rhythm after that, sorting donations and chatting about lighter things like Olivia's new workout class. The work went quickly with the two of them, and by the time they finished a couple of hours later, Sam felt like she'd really contributed.

Chapter Twenty-Three

Sam spent the rest of the day running errands, walking Arlo, and trying to lose herself in *Middlemarch*. She'd been looking forward to diving back into Dorothea's story, but she kept reading the same paragraph over and over, her mind drifting to Margaret and Gerald instead of nineteenth-century England. She ended up leaving her reading to putter around her yard, clearing away weeds and dead-heading her rose beds. At least gardening gave her hands something to do while her mind worked through the murders.

The next morning, she dressed for Margaret's memorial service. She'd let Charlotte know she was going to be there, and Charlotte, apparently still worrying over attendance, had sounded very relieved.

The Sunrise Chapel was a small, nondenominational space on the edge of downtown. It was the kind of place that hosted memorial services or weddings for people with no strong church affiliation. Sam arrived at the same time as Olivia and walked with her from the parking lot a few minutes before ten, the October morning crisp and clear.

"I hate these things," Olivia said quietly as they walked toward the entrance. "Especially when the person who died was fairly complicated."

As it turned out, Charlotte's fears about no one showing were partly justified. The chapel could hold perhaps seventy-five people, but only about twenty had gathered. Charlotte greeted them as they sat on a pew next to her. "Thanks for coming," she said, giving them a grateful look. "It means a lot. Margaret's niece flew in from Denver. I don't think she's seen Margaret in years."

Sam took in the sparse gathering. The front row held a woman in her forties who had to be the niece, sitting alone. Her posture was dutiful rather than grief-stricken. She looked like someone who was attending out of obligation rather than sorrow.

Claire Mills sat three rows back, her usual composure firmly in place, though her eyes looked tired. She gave Sam a small nod of acknowledgment. Sam noticed she'd chosen a seat near the aisle, as if ready to make a quick exit if needed.

Dylan arrived next, slipping into the back row. He wore an ill-fitting sport coat that looked borrowed, and his discomfort was palpable. He kept his head down, studying the memorial program as if it contained fascinating information.

Pamela sat near the middle, calm and composed. She wore a navy dress, her gray hair in its usual neat bun. The treasurer looked like he wasn't sure why he'd come.

There was an elderly couple there and a middle-aged woman with kind eyes.

And then there was Sofia. She sat alone on the right side, three rows from the front. She'd either wanted to avoid sitting with her cousin or didn't feel she had the right. Even from the back, Sam could see the tension in her shoulders and the way she twisted a tissue in her hands. Her dark hair fell forward, partially hiding her face.

Chief Hawkins and Detective Phillips stood near the back corner, their presence both subtle and unmistakable. Phillips' sharp eyes tracked each person who entered, noting reactions, positioning and their behavior. When his gaze landed on Sam, there was no warmth in it, just assessment.

The service itself was painfully generic. The niece stood at the front, reading from notes in an uncertain voice.

"Margaret Brennan was a dedicated educator who touched many lives through her thirty years of teaching. She had high standards for herself and for others. She was accomplished in her field." The niece paused, clearly struggling to find more personal details. "She loved literature and believed in the power of education. She will be remembered." She carefully sat down.

The vagueness of it all hung in the air. There were no warm anecdotes, funny stories, or mentions of close friends or cherished memories. Just the bare facts of a life that had been professionally successful but personally isolated.

Sam glanced around the chapel during the brief, awkward silence that followed. Claire had her eyes closed, whether in prayer or in sleep was unclear. Dylan stared at his hands. Pamela sat with perfect stillness, her expression neutral.

And Sofia's shoulders shook with silent sobs.

The minister, who'd clearly never met Margaret, led them in a generic prayer and invited anyone who wished to share memories to come forward.

No one moved.

The silence stretched uncomfortably. Charlotte half-rose from the pew as if she might say something out of sheer social obligation, but then quickly sat back down. What could she say?

Finally, Pamela stood. The retired librarian walked to the front with quiet dignity, turning to face the small group.

"Margaret and I knew each other for some time," she said, her voice steady. "She was a woman of strong convictions and impressive intellect. She set high standards and expected others to meet them." Pamela paused, seeming to choose her words carefully. "She challenged people to be better. That wasn't always comfortable, but it came from a place of believing in excellence."

It was a masterful bit of diplomacy. Her words sounded like praise while revealing nothing personal. Sam noticed Pamela's hands were completely steady. No emotion showed on her face. She could have been reading a book report. She returned to her pew, and the minister quickly moved to closing prayers, perhaps afraid of more awkward silences.

After the service, as people filed out, Sam watched the dynamics. Claire approached the niece to offer brief condolences, then moved toward the door after taking a quick, hesitant glance at Sofia, who remained seated, her face buried in her hands.

Olivia walked over to join Charlotte, while Sam headed over to where Sofia was sitting. She slid into the pew next to Sofia. "I'm so sorry for your loss."

Sofia looked up, her eyes red and swollen. For a moment she seemed confused, as if trying to place Sam in the unfamiliar environment and during a stressful morning. Then she smiled. "Sorry. Hi Sam."

"Hi there. I just wanted to make sure you were okay."

"I'm not." Sofia's voice broke. "And I don't even know why. She was terrible to me. My whole life, nothing I did was ever good enough. She criticized everything. My choices, my education, my relationships. She looked at me as a disappointment." Fresh tears spilled down her cheeks. "So why does it hurt so much that she's gone?"

"Because she was your mother," Sam said gently. "That's complicated no matter what the relationship was like."

"I joined that stupid book club to try to understand her. I wanted to see her in a different setting and maybe try to see a side of her that wasn't constantly judging me." Sofia laughed bitterly. "And you know what? She was exactly the same. She was critical of everyone and impossible to please."

They sat in silence for a moment.

Sofia gave her head a little shake as if trying to clear it out. "Sorry. I'm apparently having a tough time sorting through all these emotions. I didn't have it in me to say anything about my mom. I could see my cousin looking all self-righteous and condescending that I hadn't stood up. But I couldn't do it. I didn't know what to say. Even if I *had* known what to say, I couldn't have talked about my mother without falling apart."

"No one should be judging you right now. You just lost your mom."

Sofia took a deep breath. "My cousin did a poor job with the eulogy. I think it was better not to say anything at all." She paused. "It was nice of Pamela to speak. I wasn't expecting that, especially since she and my mother didn't seem to get along at all."

"Didn't they?" asked Sam. "When I spoke with Pamela, she acted like she didn't know your mom much at all. But during her eulogy, she sounded like she understood your mother."

Sofia gave a short laugh. "As much as anybody could understand her. But they didn't like each other, from what I could tell. During one of the meetings, I heard Mom and Pamela arguing before book club started."

"Did you catch what they were arguing about?"

"Not really. I figured it was because my mother was being impossible, as usual. But Pamela sounded pretty upset. She said something like 'you can't do this' or 'don't, Margaret.'"

Sam asked, "Did your mother say anything in response?"

"No, because they both suddenly noticed I was there. I couldn't really read Pamela's expression. My mom just looked satisfied, like she'd won something. That's when Charlotte came to the back room, and the meeting started."

Sam asked, "Did they speak to each other again during the meeting?"

"Not that I saw. Pamela sat on the opposite side of the room and left right after the meeting ended."

Sam said, "I think you should tell the police everything you remember about that book club meeting. Even details that seem small. Did you tell them anything about this?"

Sofia shook her head. "It didn't seem important at the time. My mom was always getting under people's skin. I didn't remember it again until yesterday." She stood. "Thanks for coming over. And for coming to my mom's service."

Sofia left, looking more composed than she had at the beginning of their conversation. Sam joined Olivia outside, where Charlotte was speaking with her.

Dylan called out to Charlotte as he exited the chapel, and Charlotte walked over to speak with him.

Sam said ruefully to Olivia, "I'm sure Dylan isn't eager to talk to me again anytime soon after our conversation at the community center."

"Well, he shouldn't have been posing as something he wasn't." Olivia glanced behind Sam. "Claire Mills is coming in our direction. Need to speak with her?"

"She's probably not dying to chat with me again, either."

Olivia said, "I can take the lead. I haven't spoken with anyone since the book club meeting. I should have been reaching out, but I've been dealing with my anxiety over the whole thing."

Olivia turned and smiled at Claire, motioning her over. Claire's lips tightened before she gave a return smile and headed in their direction. "Hi ladies," she said in an upbeat tone.

"How is everything going?" asked Olivia. "I've been thinking about you. I should have texted to see how you were doing."

"It's been a real mess," said Claire, blowing out a big sigh. "I can't believe Gerald is gone."

Sam noticed she didn't mention Margaret's death, despite being in the process of leaving her memorial service.

Olivia gave her a sympathetic look. "I know you two were close."

Claire nodded. "We were writing buddies. He was such a supportive guy. Gerald's probably the only reason I kept on writing after that whole thing with Margaret."

"She should never have criticized your work like that," said Olivia, frowning. "I don't like speaking ill of the dead, but everybody knows that's not the way you deliver a critique. Maybe she was just jealous of you and was trying to cut you down to size."

"You're sweet, but I don't think that was it," said Claire. "I did want to improve the manuscript, so I shouldn't have been so sensitive." She glanced at Sam. "And, of course, there was the rest of it. Margaret sabotaged my submission to a publisher."

Olivia affected surprise, although she'd known about the sabotage from Sam. "I'm so sorry."

"Yeah. It was hard. But I'm trying to move past it. What's the old expression? Get better, not bitter? That's what I'm working on. But I'm not going to lie; it's been hard. First the big mess with Margaret, which totally messed up my confidence and my self-esteem. I wasn't sure I wanted to keep on going. Then, Gerald encouraged me to keep working on my book. Losing him has been another huge setback." Claire's voice broke a little at the end, and she shook her head.

Olivia said, "You know, I'm not saying I'm a great at giving critiques, but I'd be happy to read through your book."

"Me too," said Sam.

Claire's face brightened. "You guys are the best. I don't think I'm quite ready yet to put my work out there again, but when I am, I'll be sure to check in with you. I really appreciate it."

They spoke of other things for a few minutes before heading their separate ways. Claire walked to her car, looking lighter than she had at the start of the conversation.

"She's going to be okay," Olivia said, watching her go.

"I think so too." Sam checked her phone. "I should probably head home. Arlo's been alone most of the day."

"Give him extra treats for me." Olivia gave her a quick hug.

Sam drove home, her mind turning over everything she'd learned at the memorial service. Sofia's revelation about the argument, Claire's continuing sorrow over Gerald's death.

At home, Arlo greeted her with his usual enthusiasm, doing his welcome-home dance and snuffling at her legs. Sam changed into comfortable clothes and took him for a quick walk around the neighborhood, letting the fresh air clear her head.

When they finished their walk and were heading back inside, her phone buzzed with a text from Aiden. *How was the memorial service?*

Sad. Sparsely attended. But informative. Are you free after school lets out?

Aiden wrote back. *For you? Of course. I'll run by after work.*

Chapter Twenty-Four

Sam spent the rest of the afternoon doing mundane tasks around the house with Arlo following her from room to room, "helping." She put away laundry and then settled at the kitchen table with *Middlemarch*. She was on page 512 now, deep into the middle sections where the various storylines were beginning to intersect. She was reading about Bulstrode, the respectable banker with buried secrets from his past.

Sam made careful notes. Something about this storyline felt relevant. A man who'd built a new life, a respectable reputation, all constructed on top of a past he desperately wanted to keep hidden. When someone threatened to expose him, he became dangerous. Sam added a pink tab: *Reputation as survival. Dylan?*

By the time Aiden walked up her driveway, she'd read another twenty pages and had more questions than answers about both *Middlemarch* and the murders.

He gave her a quick hug. "Long day?"

"You could say that. Memorial services are never fun, but this one felt particularly awkward. Feel like a snack?"

Aiden said, "Actually, that would be awesome. My lunch period got abbreviated by some students taking makeup tests, so I haven't had much to eat today."

Sam immediately took out cutting boards, cheese, crackers, grapes, almonds, honey, fig jam, and before she could stop herself, was arranging everything into an elaborate spread worthy of a lifestyle magazine.

Aiden watched with barely concealed amusement as she created perfect little clusters of grapes, fanned out the crackers in overlapping circles, and arranged the cheese slices at calculated intervals.

"Sam."

"Hmm?" She was concentrating on drizzling honey in an artistic zigzag pattern.

"It's just a snack."

Sam looked down at what she'd created. A charcuterie board acceptable for a dinner party. For a random weekday afternoon. While they were discussing murder.

"I think I have a problem," she admitted.

"You think?" But Aiden was smiling.

"I can't help it. I have nervous energy." She gestured helplessly at the elaborate display. "It just comes out like this. Last week I alphabetized my spice rack a couple of times. The second time was by cuisine."

"By cuisine?"

"Italian spices, then Asian, then—you know what, never mind." Sam picked up a grape and ate it, refusing to meet his eyes. "The point is, I'm aware this is excessive. I just can't seem to stop myself when I'm processing things."

Aiden grabbed a cracker topped with cheese and fig jam. "Well, your neuroses are delicious, so I'm not complaining." He popped the cracker into his mouth. "Besides, it's sort of endearing. Most people stress-eat junk food. You stress-arrange gourmet snacks."

"It's not gourmet." Sam stopped herself, laughing. "Okay, fine. It's a little gourmet. But in my defense, there are two dead people and I'm trying to figure out who killed them. That seems like a reasonable time to go overboard on cheese presentation."

"Absolutely reasonable," Aiden agreed solemnly, though his eyes were dancing mischievously. He carried the board to the kitchen table (not the dining room table, where Sam would have headed) while Sam grabbed plates and napkins. They were naturally cloth napkins she'd folded into triangles.

Arlo positioned himself strategically between their chairs, his soulful eyes tracking every piece of cheese and fruit that moved from board to mouth.

Aiden settled into his chair. "So tell me about this awkward memorial service."

Sam filled him in on the sparse attendance, the vague eulogy, Sofia's revelation about the argument between Margaret and Pamela, and Claire's grief over Gerald.

"And I keep coming back to Dylan," she said. "He has a strong motive. Actually, he has a couple of them. He would have been furious about the way Margaret made fun of him after the open mic night. But she also knew he didn't have the MFA that he said he did. He's the obvious suspect."

"But?" Aiden prompted.

"But something doesn't feel right. Margaret's murder was patient and calculated. It was poisoned coffee, not a shove down the stairs like Gerald's death. It's hard for me to picture Dylan planning something like that." She looked up at Aiden. "Have you heard anything from your contact at the station about Margaret's death? I'm making assumptions about the coffee, but I can't think how else she might have died."

"Actually, yes. I wanted to hear about the service before I told you. Mike called me this afternoon before I came over because he knew I'd taken an interest. The toxicology report came back."

Sam's pulse quickened. "What did it show?"

"Margaret's coffee was laced with crushed blood thinner tablets." Aiden's voice was quiet. "Since Margaret was already on heart medication, it caused a fatal interaction. Whoever did this knew exactly what they were doing."

Sam sat still, processing this information. "So a drug interaction."

"That's right. Mike said it was obviously calculated. Someone had knowledge of Margaret's heart medication and how it would interact with a blood thinner. The bitterness of the coffee apparently masked any taste of the crushed pills."

Something tickled at the edge of Sam's mind. It seemed like there was something familiar. Was it about drug interactions? The thought slipped away before she could catch it.

Aiden reached across the table and took her hand. "Hey. You've been going non-stop with this. Maybe you need to step back for a bit. Let your brain rest."

"I hate stepping back," said Sam wryly.

"I know." His thumb traced circles on the back of her hand. "But sometimes that's when things click into place. It's something that can happen easier when you're not forcing it."

Sam looked down at their joined hands. The gesture was becoming familiar and comfortable. When had that happened? When had Aiden shifted from just a nice neighbor to this? Someone whose presence made everything feel more manageable?

"I'm glad you're here," she said quietly.

"Me too." His voice was warm. "Though I have to admit, when you moved in, I didn't expect to spend quite so much time discussing murder investigations."

"Sorry about that."

"Don't be. It's never boring." He squeezed her hand gently. "I'm looking forward to our next date, whenever things settle down. Maybe in a week? Unless someone else dies, in which case I understand we'll need to reschedule."

"Don't jinx it." But Sam was smiling. "A week from now sounds perfect."

They were both leaning slightly across the table now, the space between them shrinking. Aiden's gaze dropped to her lips. Sam's breath caught.

Arlo barked sharply at the back door, his "someone's in my yard" alert.

They both jumped. Aiden laughed and sat back. "Arlo has terrible timing."

"The worst." Sam stood to let Arlo out, but she was smiling. Arlo took off after a squirrel in the yard. The moment had passed, but the promise of it lingered.

The next morning, Sam was folding laundry when her phone rang. Charlotte's name flashed on the screen.

"Hi, Charlotte."

Charlotte's voice was immediately apologetic. "Sam, I'm so sorry. I feel like I'm always calling to ask you to come over to the shop."

"No worries. What's going on?"

Charlotte said, "I hate to ask this, but I'm in a bind. My mom fell this morning. I'm on the way to Asheville to see her. Apparently, the hospital wants to keep her for observation."

"Oh no. Is she okay?"

Charlotte said, "She'll be fine. She did twist her ankle badly and they want to rule out a hip fracture. I left the 'closed' sign in the window at the shop, of course. But Sam, I have a delivery coming to the shop today. It's an estate sale collection I already paid for with five boxes of vintage mysteries. The driver called and said he'll be there at three and if no one's there to receive it, he'll take them back to the warehouse and charge me again to deliver them later."

Sam glanced at the clock. "I can get there, no problem."

"Would you? I know it's a huge imposition."

"Charlotte, it's fine. I'm happy to help. Life happens when we least expect it, doesn't it? How do I get in?"

Charlotte said, "The spare key is in a lockbox attached to the downspout on the left side of the building. The code is seven-two-four-one. All you need to do is to let the driver in the back entrance, make sure the boxes aren't damaged, and lock up afterwards. Please just put the key back in the lockbox when you're done."

"Got it. Don't worry about the books or the shop. Take care of your mom."

Charlotte said, "Will do. As a small thank you, could you please pick out a book of your choice to take home with you today? It'd make me feel better about everything."

"It'll be my pleasure." Sam could spend hours in the bookshop. Charlotte always carefully curated everything that was there.

Chapter Twenty-Five

Throughout the rest of the morning and into the early afternoon, Sam walked Arlo, did more housework, and paid a few bills. At about 2:30, Sam grabbed her purse and headed out the door, giving Arlo an apologetic rub on the way out. She texted Aiden on the way out to the car. *Hope school is going well today. Handling book delivery at Charlotte's shop while she's seeing her mom in Asheville. Should be over by four. Want to come over for dinner tonight?*

His reply came quickly. *Sounds perfect. Text me when you're done at the bookstore.*

Sam smiled and pocketed her phone.

Minutes later, she found a parking spot in front of Twice-Told Tales. The bookshop looked dark and closed, its cheerful window displays somehow lonely without customers inside.

She walked around to the left side of the building and found the lockbox exactly where Charlotte had described it. The code worked on the first try, and Sam retrieved the key.

The front door opened with the familiar jingle of the bell. Sam flipped on the lights and looked around. Sam made her way through the familiar aisles, breathing in the scent of paper and ink.

She unlocked the back door and propped it open with a doorstop she found nearby in preparation for the delivery driver. Then she wandered back to the front of the store to take Charlotte up on her offer and browse the shelves while she waited.

Sam was examining the mystery section's new releases when the front door's bell jingled. Sam looked up to see Pamela Cross stepping inside, a canvas tote bag over her shoulder.

Pamela's face lit up with pleased surprise. "Hi, Sam! I didn't realize Charlotte was open today. I walked past earlier and thought she was closed."

"Actually, she *is* closed. I'm just here to accept a book delivery for her. She's in Asheville, visiting her mom."

"I hope everything's all right," said Pamela, her forehead crinkled with concern.

"Her mom had a fall, but she's going to be okay."

"Sorry about the fall, but glad her mom is okay." Pamela glanced around the shop, but made no move to leave. "It's been such a stressful week for everyone. Charlotte didn't need anything else, did she? First Margaret, then Gerald." She shook her head. "I keep thinking about that memorial service. So awkward, wasn't it? No one knew quite what to say."

"It was difficult, for sure."

Pamela set her tote bag on the counter near the register. "I left that chapel as soon as I could. The whole thing just felt so tense. I've been trying ways to handle my stress, but I'm not sure it's working. I guess I'm not handling all this as well as I thought I would."

"No one is," Sam said. "It's been such a shock."

"The library at the retirement home has been a pleasant distraction. I've been spending extra time there, making sure everything's organized and helping residents find books. Reading is a real comfort during difficult times, isn't it?"

Sam's thoughts snagged on something Pamela had just said, although she couldn't quite grasp what it was. The library. Stress management.

"You mentioned trying to handle your stress," Sam said slowly. "What techniques have you been using?"

Pamela looked at her, surprised by the question. "Oh, the usual things they tell you to do online. Deep breathing, meditating, walking. Making sure I'm taking care of myself by eating properly. And I try to remember to take my medications on time." She gave a slightly embarrassed laugh. "It's not very exciting, but it helps."

Sam's mind flashed back to the retirement home's library. To Pamela mentioning her blood thinners. And then, like tumblers clicking into place in a lock, other pieces fell together. The way she'd steered every conversation away from her past with Margaret. The fact a resident at the retirement home thought Pamela had been a former teacher. Margaret's memoir mentioning 'academic circles.'

Margaret's death. Crushed pills in coffee.

Sam must have made some sound, or her expression must have changed, because Pamela went very still.

"Sam?" Pamela's voice was uncertain. "Are you all right?"

Sam tried to keep her features neutral, but she could feel the color draining from her face. She looked at Pamela, really looked at her, and saw the exact moment when Pamela recognized what had just happened.

Pamela's expression shifted. The warmth drained away, replaced by something watchful and wary. "You just figured something out." It wasn't a question. "I can see it on your face."

Sam took an involuntary step backward.

"It was the medication comment, wasn't it?" Pamela's voice was quiet, almost sad. "I shouldn't have mentioned it. But I wasn't thinking. I was just making conversation. I guess I'm not very good at this." She paused. "Though I suppose it doesn't matter now. You've already put everything together."

Sam's heart hammered in her chest. They were alone in the closed bookshop. Her phone was in her purse, which she'd set down somewhere near the mystery section. She tried to remember exactly where without giving away her intentions by looking around for it.

"Pamela," Sam started.

"The problem is that I can't have you telling anyone. They won't understand. Not the police or anyone else."

Sam didn't answer. She took another step back, trying to angle toward the center aisle that would lead to either the front door or the back entrance.

"I didn't want to do any of this." Pamela's voice cracked slightly. "You have to understand that. I just wanted Margaret to stop. For her to leave me alone. I didn't want her to publish those lies about me."

The betrayal in academic circles that Margaret's memoir had been referencing.

"What lies?" Sam asked carefully, still backing away.

Pamela's laugh was bitter. "In her memoir. She was writing about our time at the university together. We were both graduate students, working on our dissertations in Victorian literature. I was finishing my PhD. Margaret was further along. We'd discuss our research over coffee and share ideas the way colleagues do. I thought she was helping me."

"So this was some time ago. How was Margaret back then? Was she just as difficult?" All Sam could think about was buying time.

"Margaret was actually pretty fun back then. She was super smart and I loved getting her perspective. But when she published, it was my framework."

Sam asked, "She'd stolen your work?"

Pamela nodded. "It was my analysis of how Victorian women writers subverted narratives through domestic fiction. When I confronted Margaret, she claimed I'd stolen from *her*. Can you imagine?"

"Did you tell the English department chair what happened?"

Pamela said, "Of course I did. They investigated and sided with her. Naturally. She'd ingratiated herself with the entire department while I'd been focused on my research. I was a nobody, just an assistant professor who'd never published anything significant." Pamela's hands shook. "They suggested I quietly resign before my tenure review. They said it would be better for everyone. So I left academia entirely and became a librarian. I had to rebuild my whole life from nothing."

"I'm so sorry this happened to you."

Pamela's eyes filled with tears. "Margaret destroyed my entire future. And she was going to do it again with her memoir. She said the publisher wanted it by spring. I had maybe four months." Her voice rose. "She was going to call me a liar in her memoir. Margaret would paint herself as the victim when she was the one who stole from me."

Sam's mind was racing, pieces clicking into place. Not just the memoir, but the *method*. She said, "At the book club, the first meeting I went to, Margaret talked about the previous month's book. It was *The Cardiac Protocol*, I think. She mentioned she was on three different heart medications." Sam's voice was steady now, certain. "You knew that."

Pamela shrugged. "She told everyone at that book club meeting. Margaret loved being the expert on everything, even her own medical conditions."

"I've been reading the next month's selection. *Middlemarch*." It sounded absurd, even as she spoke the words. "The book Margaret chose. There's this character, Bulstrode. He's built this respectable life, but it's all constructed on top of buried secrets from his past. And then someone threatens to expose his past and destroy the reputation he's spent decades building."

"Stop," Pamela whispered.

"Bulstrode can't let it happen. The threat of exposure, of having everyone know what really happened twenty years ago, was horrifying to him." Sam took a deep breath. "You couldn't let Margaret make those lies permanent, in her memoir. You'd already rebuilt your whole life once before."

"She was going to publish it," Pamela said, her voice breaking. "Everyone would read Margaret's version of events. Those lies about me plagiarizing *her* work when she was the one who stole from me." She stopped. "I spent twenty years being the bigger person. I couldn't let her make those lies permanent."

"So you put blood thinner in her coffee. You knew, from what Margaret had said, that it would interact with her heart medication."

Pamela's eyes filled with tears. "I didn't want to hurt anyone. I just wanted her to stop."

Sam thought about Bulstrode, how George Eliot had shown the way one desperate act led to another, how trying to protect a secret could destroy everything.

"I can only imagine how hurt you must have been by what Margaret did to you. And how you must have felt when she stole your work."

Pamela's laugh was bitter. "Hurt? I was completely erased. Everything I'd worked for was gone. And she got tenure, the publication, and all the respect. She built her whole career on my research." She wiped angrily at her eyes. "But I never meant for Gerald to get hurt. Never. I didn't know he'd seen me. I panicked."

Sam's back hit a bookshelf. She'd unconsciously been retreating and now was near the history section, halfway between the front and back of the shop. "Pamela, it's not too late to talk with the authorities about this. It's better that way."

"Not too late?" Pamela's voice sharpened. "I've killed two people, Sam. There's no coming back from that." Her gaze focused on Sam with sudden intensity. "Have you told anyone? Really, I need to know. Have you talked to the police?"

Sam tried to answer, but when she opened her mouth, no sound emerged.

Pamela closed her eyes briefly. When she opened them, something had changed. It was a hardening, as if she'd made a decision. She moved toward the counter near the register, where Charlotte kept supplies for opening boxes and processing new inventory.

Sam saw Pamela's hand close around a heavy brass bookend shaped like an owl. She remembered it was part of a pair Charlotte used to display new releases in the front window.

"I'm sorry," Pamela said, her voice breaking. "I'm so sorry, Sam. You seem like a genuinely good person. But I can't go to prison and have everyone know what I've done. Margaret's already taken so much from me. I'm not going to have her take my freedom, too."

Chapter Twenty-Six

Sam's mind raced. The back door was closer than the front, and it was propped open for the delivery. The delivery must be running behind. If she could just get past Pamela.

"Please don't make this harder," Pamela said, moving to block the center aisle. Tears streamed down her face, but her grip on the bookend didn't waver. "I don't want to hurt you. But I can't let you tell."

Sam grabbed a hardcover from the shelf behind her and threw it. The book sailed past Pamela's shoulder. Sam had never been great at throwing and missed her target in a big way, but it did make Pamela duck instinctively.

Sam ran.

She dodged left, into the literature section, then cut right toward the back of the shop. Behind her, she heard Pamela's footsteps, faster than she would have expected for a woman in her sixties.

"Sam, please!" Pamela's voice was desperate. "Stop!"

Sam's hip clipped the corner of a display table, sending paperbacks cascading to the floor. She caught her balance and kept going, the back hallway in sight now, the rectangle of daylight from the propped-open door.

A male voice called from the back entrance: "Hello? Delivery for Charlotte Webb?"

Sam nearly sobbed with relief. "Here! I'm here."

She burst into the back hallway just as a young man in a delivery uniform came through the door, pushing a dolly loaded with boxes. He looked startled at her appearance—breathless, wild-eyed.

Behind her, she heard Pamela stop abruptly, still holding the bookend aloft.

Sam turned. Pamela's face was white, her expression stricken. For a long moment, their eyes met.

"Ma'am?" The delivery driver looked between them, confused. "Is everything okay here?"

Pamela's gaze moved from Sam to the driver, then back to Sam. In that moment, Sam saw the full weight of everything crashing down on Pamela's face. The murders, the years of bitterness, and the impossible situation she'd created for herself.

The bookend fell from Pamela's hands with a heavy thud against the floor.

Then Pamela ran, not toward them but away, back through the bookshop toward the front entrance.

"Call 911!" Sam told the driver, already moving after Pamela. "Tell them there's been an attempted assault and the suspect is fleeing."

The driver fumbled for his phone as Sam ran through the shop. She reached the front just in time to see Pamela burst through the door, the bell jangling violently. Sam stopped in the doorway, not chasing, just watching.

Pamela ran onto the sidewalk and directly into Main Street without looking.

The screech of brakes pierced the afternoon air.

Sam's stomach dropped. She saw it happen as if in slow motion. Pamela's body collided with the front panel of a sedan, the sickening thump of impact. Pamela spun and fell to the pavement.

The car wasn't going fast. Main Street had a 25-mile-per-hour speed limit, and the driver had been approaching the stop sign at the corner. But it was fast enough.

Sam ran into the street. The driver, a middle-aged woman, was already out of the car, her hands over her mouth, making a keening sound of horror.

Pamela lay on the pavement near the centerline. She was conscious, curled on her side, making small sounds of pain. Blood trickled from a cut on her forehead, and her left leg was bent at an unnatural angle.

"Don't move," Sam said, kneeling beside her. She was afraid to move her for fear she'd make things worse. "Help is coming."

"I'm sorry," Pamela whispered. Her face was wet with tears. "I'm sorry, sorry, sorry."

A small crowd had gathered on the sidewalk. Sam heard someone say they'd called an ambulance, someone else asking what happened, another voice asking to give them space.

"She just ran out," the driver was saying, her voice shaking. "She didn't even look. I didn't see her until she was right there. I tried to stop. I did."

"It wasn't your fault," someone told her. "We saw it. She just ran right out."

Sam heard sirens in the distance, growing closer. She stayed kneeling beside Pamela, who had closed her eyes and was breathing in short, pained gasps.

A car pulled up abruptly at the curb. It wasn't a police car, but Aiden's Subaru. He got out quickly, his expression alarmed as he took in the scene: a woman on the ground, the damaged car, the crowd, and Sam kneeling in the street.

"Sam!" He reached her in just a few strides. "What happened? Are you hurt?"

Sam looked up at him. "I'm okay. I'm not hurt." Her voice wavered. "Pamela tried to kill me. She's the one who killed Margaret and Gerald. Then she ran, and the car . . ."

His arms came around her, carefully pulling her to her feet and away from Pamela as the EMTs approached.

"You're safe," Aiden said quietly, one hand cupping the back of her head. "You're safe now."

Sam let herself lean against him for a moment, breathing in the familiar scent of his soap. Then she pulled back slightly as two police cruisers and an unmarked car approached.

"I need to talk to Lieutenant Phillips," she said. "I need to tell him everything." She paused. "Aiden, could you do me a favor? Can you meet the delivery driver in the bookstore? He's trying to drop off a delivery for Charlotte. And can you make sure he gives a statement to the police? He was a witness."

He nodded. "On it."

The next thirty minutes passed in a blur of activity. Paramedics loaded Pamela onto a stretcher. Sam overheard one of them say something about a possible broken femur and concussion. They took her away with a police escort.

Lieutenant Phillips listened with an increasingly grim expression as Sam explained the confrontation in the bookshop, Pamela's confession, and her dash into traffic.

The delivery driver corroborated Sam's account, describing how he'd found her running from a woman holding a heavy object aloft. Other witnesses confirmed Pamela had bolted blindly into the street. When Phillips finally said Sam could go, Aiden retrieved her purse from the bookshop, locked up properly, and put the key back in the lockbox.

"Come on," he said gently, guiding her toward his car. "I'm taking you home."

Chapter Twenty-Seven

Sam didn't argue. Her legs felt shaky, and she realized her hands were trembling.

Arlo greeted them at the door with his usual enthusiasm, completely unaware of how close his human had come to serious harm. Sam sank onto her sofa while Aiden locked the door behind them and then disappeared into her kitchen.

He returned with a glass of water and a throw blanket, which he draped gently over her shoulders.

"Thank you," Sam said quietly.

Aiden sat beside her, close enough that their shoulders touched. "Do you want to talk about it? Or would you rather just relax and be quiet for a while?"

Sam considered. The events at the bookshop felt both surreal and far too real at the same time. "Pamela was just a sad, angry person who'd been hurt and never got past it. And she killed two people because of it."

Aiden nodded.

Sam said, "I can't help feeling sorry for her. Margaret stole her research, took credit, then destroyed her academic career. It was awful. But it just doesn't justify murder."

"No," Aiden agreed. "It doesn't."

They sat in silence for a moment. Then Aiden said, "You said she tried to kill you."

"She had a heavy bookend." Sam stopped, the image too clear in her mind. "If that driver hadn't arrived when he did, it could have been a totally different ending."

Aiden's jaw tightened. He reached for her hand, lacing his fingers through hers. "But he did arrive. You're safe."

Sam squeezed his hand, grateful for the solid warmth. "I threw a book at her," she said and was surprised to hear herself laugh. It was a slightly hysterical sound. "I have truly awful aim. I missed by about two feet."

"I'll take you out to the batting cages," Aiden said, his tone serious, but his eyes warm. "We'll work on that."

Sam laughed again, more naturally this time. Then, without thinking too hard about it, she leaned her head against his shoulder.

He went still for a moment, then shifted slightly so she'd be more comfortable. His free hand came up to rest gently against her hair.

"I'm glad you happened by when you did," Sam said quietly. "I needed to see a friendly face."

"I always take Main Street on my way home from school," Aiden said. "I saw the crowd and the woman in the road. Then I saw you." He paused. "I've never been so scared in my life."

Sam lifted her head to look at him.

"I'm okay," she said softly. "Really."

"I know." But he didn't move away. "Sam, I—"

Sam's phone rang, shattering the moment. She pulled back and fumbled for it in her purse. The screen showed Lieutenant Phillips's number.

"I should take this," she said apologetically. "It's Phillips."

Aiden nodded and stood, giving her space. "I'll make some coffee."

Sam answered the phone. "Lieutenant Phillips."

"Ms. Prescott." Phillps's voice was grave but not unkind. "I wanted to update you on Ms. Cross's condition and let you know what happens next."

"How is Pamela?" Sam asked.

"Broken femur, concussion, some bruising and lacerations. The doctors say she'll recover fully, though the leg will require surgery." He paused. "She's been lucid since arriving at the hospital. She confessed to both murders and the attempt on your life. She gave a full statement."

Sam closed her eyes briefly. "Both murders."

"Margaret Brennan and Gerald Parker. She confirmed she used crushed blood thinner tablets in Dr. Brennan's coffee. She was on warfarin herself for a heart condition, so she had ready access."

"What about Gerald Parker?"

Phillips's tone shifted slightly. "She says he didn't realize he'd witnessed her near Dr. Brennan's coffee. He'd told her he didn't understand what he was seeing at the time. He'd thought maybe Pamela was helping Margaret out by adding cream or sugar. But after Dr. Brennan died, the more he thought about it, the more it worried him. He'd apparently called Ms. Cross and asked her about it, thinking maybe there was just an innocent explanation."

"I see."

Phillips added, "Ms. Cross seemed genuinely distraught over Mr. Parker's death. She said she never meant for anyone else to get hurt."

"But she was willing to hurt me," Sam said quietly.

"Yes." Phillips didn't soften it.

"What happens to Pamela now?"

Phillips said, "Once she's stable enough, she'll be arrested and formally charged with two counts of murder and one count of attempted murder. Her attorney has already indicated she intends to plead guilty."

After they hung up, Sam sat staring at her phone. Aiden returned to the sofa, but he didn't sit as close as before. He seemed uncertain, as if the interrupted moment had made him second-guess himself.

"She confessed to everything," Sam said. "She'll plead guilty."

Aiden nodded. "That's good. Clear resolution." He rubbed the back of his neck. "Listen, I should probably let you rest. You've been through a lot today."

"Don't go." The words came out before Sam could think about them. "Please. I don't want to be alone right now."

His expression softened. "Are you sure? I don't want to—"

"I'm sure." Sam pulled the blanket more tightly around her shoulders. "But I'm terrible company right now. I'm shaky, and I can't promise I'll make good conversation."

"I don't need good conversation." Aiden settled back onto the sofa. "I just need to know you're okay."

Chapter Twenty-Eight

Two days after the confrontation at the bookshop, Sam received a text from Charlotte. *Book club meeting at the shop tonight, 7pm. Nothing formal, just us. Please come if you're up to it.*

Sam responded right away, accepting the invite. She wanted to dispel the bad feelings she had from her last moments in Twice-Told Tales with better memories.

When she arrived later that day, she found the core group gathered in the shop. "How's your mom?" Sam asked Charlotte.

"Stable," she said with a smile. "Thanks. She's in a physical therapy rehab facility for ten days or so."

Charlotte had ordered pizza for everyone, and Claire, Dylan, Sofia, and Olivia were there. The atmosphere was subdued but warm.

They all settled into seats in the back room with their food and drinks. Charlotte cleared her throat. "I've been thinking about what we want to do moving forward. About book club."

"I think we all love the book club," said Olivia, glancing around at everyone, looking for agreement. There were lots of bobbed heads.

"Even when Margaret was being impossible," said Dylan wryly. "Seriously, this club keeps me going sometimes."

Sofia said quietly, "I came to this club looking for something totally different. Really, I guess, just trying to figure out my mom. I didn't succeed at that, but I really enjoyed connecting with all of you."

Claire hopped into the discussion. "I hate to let what happened destroy something we all got a lot of enjoyment and satisfaction from. Let's keep meeting. The same group. If everyone's comfortable with that."

There was a murmur of agreement around the room.

Charlotte smiled. "Then that's settled. Thanks so much, everybody. I always look forward to the books and discussions. It's always one of the highlights of my month."

Dylan shifted in his seat. "So are we still doing *Middlemarch*? Because I have to say that book is seriously humbling me."

A ripple of laughter went through the group.

"How far are you?" Sofia asked.

"Page 127." Dylan grimaced. "Of 880. And I'm reading like my life depends on it."

"I'm at page 610," Sam admitted, pulling out her heavily tabbed copy from her purse. Several members stared at her sticky tabs.

"Of course you are," Olivia said fondly.

Claire laughed. "I'm at 290, and I have to say that Margaret knew what she was doing when she picked this one. Stick with it. It's challenging, but brilliant."

"The prose is beautiful," Sofia agreed. "I'm only on page 180, but I'm taking my time with it." She grinned. "My mom would have eviscerated us for not being further along."

"She always had lots of opinions," said Claire with a smile.

Charlotte said, "Margaret would have read it twice by now and annotated every page."

Sam looked down at her purple-penned notes. "She'd probably have loved that someone in this group actually made character index cards."

"You made character index cards?" Dylan asked.

"There are lots of characters," said Sam in self-defense.

"My mother would definitely have approved," Sofia said gently. "She believed in taking books seriously."

"Even when she was impossible about it," Dyland added. But his voice was warm now, not bitter.

Claire raised her water glass. "To Margaret. Who challenged us, infuriated us, and made us better readers, whether we wanted to be or not."

They all raised their drinks—water, tea, or soft drinks. "To Margaret," they echoed.

"And to *Middlemarch*," Dylan said. "Which I am absolutely going to finish, if only so Margaret can haunt me less judgmentally."

Claire said, "On a different topic. I did speak with Gerald's wife. She's planning a memorial service for Gerald and asked if we could all come. She said he loved books and good conversation. And she said she hoped our club would continue on. She said Gerald wouldn't want us to stop."

"So it's settled," said Charlotte with a smile. "Thanks, everybody."

There was a pause where the group seemed to be deep in their own individual thoughts.

"I keep thinking about Pamela," Olivia said. "All that anger she must have been carrying all these years. It's just so sad. It doesn't excuse what she did. But it just feels tragic."

They talked it all out for another hour, sharing their memories of Gerald, amazed at his being Geraldine Hartwell. They talked about Margaret's sharp intelligence despite her difficult personality. It felt like a kind of closure to Sam.

After the meeting finally broke up and as Sam was leaving, Charlotte pulled her aside. "I'm so sorry about what happened at the bookshop. If I'd known, I'd never have put you in the position of waiting for the delivery."

"You couldn't have known," Sam said. "And your mom needed you. How is she doing with the rehab program?"

"Better. The doctor says she's getting stronger every day and might go back home next week." Charlotte squeezed Sam's hand. "But I keep thinking about you being there alone with Pamela." Her voice caught, and she shook her head.

"I'm okay," Sam said. "Really. The delivery driver showed up at exactly the right moment. Even if he hadn't, I feel like I could have gotten away from Pamela once I'd gotten out that back door."

"Still." Charlotte's eyes were damp. "You're my friend, Sam. The thought of something happening to you in my shop just hurts me."

Sam hugged her. "I'm fine. Everyone's going to be fine."

Sam had just gotten home from the book club meeting when her phone buzzed. Aiden's message said: *How are you doing?*

She smiled and typed back: *Home from book club. Want to come over? Fair warning: I'm planning popcorn and a romcom to escape reality.*

The three dots appeared. *Be there in 20.*

When Aiden arrived, he had a bag of peanut M&M's. "For the popcorn," he explained. He wore a careful expression that suggested he was still trying to figure out where they stood.

Sam took the candy and gestured him inside. "Thanks for checking in on me. I know it's been a weird few days."

"Weird is one word for it." Aiden followed her to the living room, where Arlo immediately demanded attention. "How was book club?"

"Good, actually. Sad sometimes, but good. We're going to keep meeting." Sam headed to the kitchen and pulled out the popcorn. "And we'll be at Gerald's memorial."

"Good." Aiden leaned against the kitchen doorway, watching her. "And you're really okay? Not just saying it?"

Sam paused, the popcorn bag in her hand. "I'm getting there. I keep replaying the moment I realized it was Pamela. And the look on her face when she had that bookend." She shook her head. "But I'm okay. Especially when I have distractions." She held up the popcorn. "Hence the romcom and popcorn plan."

"What are we watching?"

Sam said, "I was thinking *You've Got Mail*. Classic, charming, zero murders."

"Perfect." Aiden smiled.

They settled on the sofa, a bowl of popcorn and M&M's between them, and Arlo sprawled across both their feet. The movie started, and for a while they just watched in comfortable silence.

But about halfway through, Sam found her attention drifting from the screen to Aiden's profile; she noted the way he smiled at the funny parts, the way his hair was slightly rumpled from his day at school, and the simple fact he'd dropped everything to be with her.

"You're not watching," he observed, glancing over at her.

"No," Sam admitted. "I'm not."

"Is the movie not working as a distraction?"

"The movie's fine." Sam set the popcorn bowl on the coffee table. "I was just thinking about when you started to say something to me, before Phillips called and interrupted us."

Aiden's expression grew cautious. "I remember."

"What were you going to say?"

He was quiet for a moment, and Sam could see him choosing his words carefully. "I was going to say that I care about you. A lot. And seeing you in danger made me realize I should probably stop pretending I'm content with us just being friends."

Sam's heart hammered in her chest. "What if I said I'm not content with that either?"

His eyes widened slightly. "Then I'd ask if you're saying that because you mean it, or because you just had a traumatic experience."

"I'm saying it because I mean it." Sam shifted closer to him. "I've meant it for a while now. I just wasn't sure about getting into another relationship again. But now I am."

Aiden smiled. "I've been half in love with you since I met you."

"Half in love?"

"Maybe more than half," admitted Aiden.

Arlo, apparently deciding this had gone on long enough without him, jumped onto the couch and wedged himself between them, his tail wagging furiously.

Aiden laughed and scratched behind Arlo's ears. "I think we have a chaperone."

"He's very protective." Sam settled back against the sofa, and this time when Aiden put his arm around her shoulders, it felt natural. Right.

They finished the movie that way—Sam tucked against Aiden's side, Arlo sprawled across their laps.

The following week, Lieutenant Phillips called with a final update.

"Pamela Cross gave us the full background. Ms. Cross accused Margaret Brennan of plagiarism, then Margaret counterclaimed Ms. Cross was trying to steal from her. When the department investigated," Phillips's tone was neutral, "they sided with Margaret. Ms. Cross was pressured to resign and left academia completely, never finishing her PhD dissertation."

"Did she actually steal the research?" Sam asked quietly.

"We'll never know for certain. The university records show competing claims, with no definitive proof either way. But Margaret Brennan had the reputation and the connections and Ms. Cross had none of that." He paused. "And it certainly appeared Ms. Cross thought she was wronged. She saw Margaret's memoir as the final humiliation, making the accusations permanent and public."

Phillips went on to say that Pamela Cross had been formally charged and had pleaded guilty to two counts of second-degree murder and one count of attempted murder. Her attorney was working on a plea deal, but she would go to prison. The only question was for how long.

Despite everything, she couldn't help feeling a thread of sympathy for the woman who'd let twenty years of anger destroy her life and take two others.

Life in Sunset Ridge continued as usual. Nora's relationship with Harold continued to develop. They'd moved from coffee dates to actual dinners, and Nora seemed genuinely happy and a lot less nosy about her neighbors' business. Most of the time, at least. Olivia adopted Marmalade and sent Sam at least a dozen photos a day of the orange cat happily sleeping in various sunny spots. The book club attended the memorial for Gerald, sharing memories with his wife.

And Sam continued her work volunteering, walking Arlo twice a day, and meeting Aiden for dinner at least twice a week. They took things slowly and carefully. Life had a way of moving forward.

And sometimes, if you were very lucky, it moved forward into something better than what had come before.

About the Author

Bestselling cozy mystery author Elizabeth Spann Craig is a library-loving, avid mystery reader. A pet-owning Southerner, her four series are full of cats, corgis, and cheese grits. The mother of two, she lives with her husband, a fun-loving corgi, and a couple of cute cats.

Sign up for Elizabeth's free newsletter to stay updated on releases:

https://bit.ly/2xZUXqO

This and That

I love hearing from my readers. You can find me on Facebook as Elizabeth Spann Craig Author, on Twitter as elizabethscraig, on my website at elizabethspanncraig.com, and by email at elizabethspanncraig@gmail.com.

Thanks so much for reading my book…I appreciate it. If you enjoyed the story, would you please leave a short review on the site where you purchased it? Just a few words would be great. Not only do I feel encouraged reading them, but they also help other readers discover my books. Thank you!

Did you know my books are available in print and ebook formats? Most of the Myrtle Clover series is available in audio and some of the Southern Quilting mysteries are. Find the audiobooks here: https://elizabethspanncraig.com/audio/

Please follow me on BookBub for my reading recommendations and release notifications.

I'd also like to thank some folks who helped me put this book together. Thanks to my cover designer, Karri Klawiter, for her awesome covers. Thanks to my editor, Judy Beatty for her help. Thanks to beta readers Amanda Arrieta, Rebecca Wahr, Cassie Kelley, and Dan Harris for all of their helpful suggestions and careful reading. Thanks to my ARC readers for helping to spread the word. Thanks, as always, to my family and readers.

Other Works by Elizabeth

Myrtle Clover Series in Order (be sure to look for the Myrtle series in audio, ebook, and print):

Pretty is as Pretty Dies

Progressive Dinner Deadly

A Dyeing Shame

A Body in the Backyard

Death at a Drop-In

A Body at Book Club

Death Pays a Visit

A Body at Bunco

Murder on Opening Night

Cruising for Murder

Cooking is Murder

A Body in the Trunk

Cleaning is Murder

Edit to Death

Hushed Up

A Body in the Attic

Murder on the Ballot

Death of a Suitor

A Dash of Murder
Death at a Diner
A Myrtle Clover Christmas
Murder at a Yard Sale
Doom and Bloom
A Toast to Murder
Mystery Loves Company
A Murder Down Memory Lane
Murder Sees All

THE VILLAGE LIBRARY Mysteries in Order:
Checked Out
Overdue
Borrowed Time
Hush-Hush
Where There's a Will
Frictional Characters
Spine Tingling
A Novel Idea
End of Story
Booked Up
Out of Circulation
Shelf Life
Dead Silence
Plot Twist (2026)
The Sunset Ridge Mysteries in Order
The Type-A Guide to Solving Murder

The Type-A Guide to Dinner Parties
The Type-A Guide to Book Clubs
Southern Quilting Mysteries in Order:
Quilt or Innocence
Knot What it Seams
Quilt Trip
Shear Trouble
Tying the Knot
Patch of Trouble
Fall to Pieces
Rest in Pieces
On Pins and Needles
Fit to be Tied
Embroidering the Truth
Knot a Clue
Quilt-Ridden
Needled to Death
A Notion to Murder
Crosspatch
Behind the Seams
Quilt Complex
A Southern Quilting Cozy Christmas

MEMPHIS BARBEQUE MYSTERIES in Order (Written as Riley Adams):
Delicious and Suspicious
Finger Lickin' Dead

Hickory Smoked Homicide

Rubbed Out

And a standalone "cozy zombie" novel: Race to Refuge, written as Liz Craig